THE HOUSE ON TURNER LANE

James R. Nelson

Prologue

FOREST RANGER CHARLIE Loonsfoot slammed on the brakes as he rounded a steep corner on South Boundary Road. Two black bear cubs scrambled out of his way and played next to an outcrop of rock. By the size of them, they were probably around seven months old and both males. They were born in January when their mother was still in hibernation.

Charlie watched as they wrestled with each other. He peered out of his rain-spotted windshield. Where was she? Close. Mama wouldn't be far from her cubs. They'd better enjoy their time with her now because next summer she'd be snapping at them to go off on their own.

He hit the gas pedal and continued up the steep road. It was nice to get out of that damn office. He was proud of his promotion, but now it kept him behind a desk most of the time. He pulled into an overlook area and turned up the heater, but he knew it was no use. The government truck he grabbed from the motor pool had problems. He rubbed his hands together and flipped on the two-way radio. Nothing urgent. Just typical chatter. Not much was going on. The cold front and rain squalls that rolled in a few days before were enough to nearly empty the park. It sure didn't feel like July.

1

The two cubs he'd seen, and probably about two thousand other bears that roamed the 60,000 acre Porcupine Mountain Wilderness State Park, had the place almost to themselves.

He rubbed condensation off his window and looked outside. There was nothing to see. A gray mist hung over the mountains.

Back down the road, one of the bear cubs stopped and sniffed the air. He walked closer to a flat spot fifty feet off the pavement where the ground had been disturbed. He pawed at the dirt a few times and then dug deeper. Curious, his sibling wandered over and joined in. The glint of a thin gold necklace was ignored as the rancid smell of decay captured their attention.

Slowly they uncovered a human skull and pried it from the ground. The first cub batted it and chased after it as it rolled down an incline. His brother ran over, bit down between the eye sockets, and tried to yank the skull away.

From a dense thicket their mother gave a sharp bark. The two cubs released their newly found toy and scampered toward her. The dropped skull rolled down a small hill and splashed into a fast-moving creek where it bobbed along the surface for a few minutes before sinking. The strong current carried it downstream tumbling unseen from the surface, among the stones and gravel of the creek bed.

Chapter 1

OLIVIA THOMPSON BRUSHED away tears as she slipped out of her mother's bedroom and quietly closed the door behind her. She sat down at the kitchen table. "I hope it's my imagination, Elaine, but I think Mom looks even thinner now than she did when I got home from college." She picked up a napkin and dabbed her eyes.

"I don't think so. They've been monitoring her weight every time I take her to the clinic. It may have gone down a little, but Doctor Franz thinks things have actually started to stabilize."

Olivia reached over and took Elaine's hand. "What would we do without you?"

"Just stop now. Your mother and I have been best friends ever since your family moved here." She smiled. "You girls were so adorable. Just think, you were only three and your sister was almost six." She stared at Olivia. "Look at you now. A whole year of college behind you."

Olivia glanced at the clock above the stove. "Speaking of Rachel, why isn't she here?"

Elaine sighed. "I think she's having a hard time facing the fact that your mother's sick. She…she seems to think this is going to go away somehow."

Olivia went over to the coffeepot. "You want a refill?"

"Sure." Elaine handed her a cup.

Olivia poured them both coffee and sat back down. "You're making excuses for her just like Mom always does. She has a hard time facing anything. Getting a job, keeping a job, getting a boyfriend, keeping a boyfriend…" She took a sip. "I'm sorry. I shouldn't vent. But while I was gone, she should've been over here doing all the things you've been doing. Sometimes I…I just don't understand her."

"I'm over here doing things I want to be doing. If it was me, you know your mother would be at my place doing the same things I'm doing for her." She picked up her cup. "Remember when your dad got sick? Rachel didn't handle that very well either. She was shocked when your father finally passed. Everyone else saw it coming."

Olivia dabbed her eyes again. "You're being too kind. Rachel was always too busy with her own issues to worry about Dad. She's self-centered. That's all there is to it." She brushed a lock of hair away from her face. Maybe that's why they were never close.

She picked up her cellphone and punched in a number. "Rachel, it's three-thirty. You were supposed to be here at three. Are you on your way?" Her face tightened. "Maybe tomorrow? That's your answer?" After another minute, she ended the call and set the phone back down.

During the conversation, Elaine had left the table and was busying herself straightening up the kitchen.

"I hate to ask," Olivia said, "but can you stay another hour?"

4

"Sure. I need to be home at five when Ben gets there, but dinners already in the Crock Pot."

Olivia grabbed her purse. "I need to have a little talk with my sister. You know, face to face."

As she drove down North Street, Olivia was surprised to see how many more businesses were closed since the last time she'd visited her sister. Once the docks shut down and the huge ore boats stopped coming, the many bars that lined the street just couldn't make it. Was Beamer's Tavern still open? Just like Rachel to live above a bar.

When Olivia rounded the corner, she had her answer. Several cars were in the parking lot, and music blasted from inside. She climbed halfway up the old wooden steps to her sister's apartment and then stopped in panic. The handrail she was holding onto swayed back and forth. It felt like the whole staircase could collapse at any minute. How could Rachel live here?

Olivia caught her breath and carefully climbed the rest of the way to her sister's door. She knocked. There was no answer. She knocked again, then peeked into a side window. Dirty dishes were stacked on the kitchen counter. Was Rachel out somewhere?

Olivia turned and cautiously made her way back down the rickety staircase. She passed the door to the tavern and stopped. Could Rachel be inside? She pressed her face close to the big plate glass window. Yes, there she was having a drink at the bar. Olivia entered the building and took a seat next to her.

Rachel turned to her in surprise. "What are you doing here? Out slummin'?" She motioned to the bartender. "Hey, Gene, get my sister a drink. Put it on my tab."

Olivia reached into her purse and tossed some money on the bar. "I'll pay for my own drink, thank you."

"What are you having?" the bartender asked.

"Cabernet Sauvignon, please."'

Rachel's eyebrows arched. "Did you hear that? Cabernet Sauvignon." She looked down the length of the bar. "We're all drinking Bud Lite, but the queen here wants Cabernet Sauvignon."

Ignoring her sister's comment, Olivia replied, "It's nice to see you too. I've been home three weeks now, and I've only seen you a few times."

"I've been…busy." Rachel pulled a cigarette from a pack on the bar and lit it.

Olivia waved the smoke away. "Mom was looking forward to seeing you today."

"Really? The last time I was over there all she did was sleep. When she finally did wake up, all she did was talk about how happy she was that you were home."

"Elaine from next door is helping out a lot. I thought that, since you're not working, and I'm home now, we could both figure out a schedule and let Elaine get back to doing her own things."

Rachel grimaced. "A schedule? Don't sign me up for any schedule. I've been looking for a job. It's not easy finding something around here. When an opening does come up, I've gotta jump on it. I can't be tied down to any schedule."

Olivia stood. "That's what I thought you'd say." She turned toward the door.

Rachel looked at Olivia's glass. It was still three-fourth's full. "What about your drink?"

Olivia didn't respond. She continued walking toward the entrance.

"Suit yourself." Rachel picked up the glass and chugged the wine.

Chapter 2

OLIVIA CARRIED THE lunch tray into her mother's room and gently set it down on the table next to the bed. "You're looking better, Mom. You have more color than you did the last few days. Are you ready for some lunch?"

Joyce Thompson slowly pushed herself up to a sitting position. "I do feel better. And for the first time in weeks, I'm actually hungry." She looked over at the tray. "Let me start with the apple slices. They look good."

Olivia smiled and handed her the small plate of fruit. "Here. I'm so happy I don't have to argue and try to convince you to eat something."

Joyce took a bite. "The doctor said I should be starting to feel better soon. I didn't think it would take so long." Her mother slowly ate more of her lunch.

Olivia sat back in amazement. She was eating better than she had since Olivia returned from college. She couldn't wait to tell Elaine.

Her mother patted her lips with a napkin. "I heard you talking to your boyfriend this morning. He's been calling you a lot lately. I think this is more serious than you've let on."

Olivia shook her head. "No, I guess he just misses me, that's all."

"You haven't told me much about him. What's his name?"

"That's because we haven't gone out that many times. I only met him about a month before school got out. His name's Thomas. Thomas Riggins."

"Based on all the times he calls you, I think you must have made quite an impression on the young man."

"Please, Mother." She needed to change the subject. "He's not a young man. He was a Marine, and he's going to school on the GI Bill."

Joyce looked up. "How old is he?"

Olivia thought. "I'd say he's in his late twenties."

"How did you meet him?"

"He knew one of my girlfriends. They went to high school together. I met him down in the student union, and we kind of hit it off."

"Does he want to come by and see you? If he does, why don't you have him over?"

"He's going up to the mountains to do some hiking, and he wants me to go with him."

Joyce turned. "You should go."

Olivia sat back. "But I want to be here with you."

Joyce reached over and patted her daughter's hand. "Thank you. I know you do. But you have a life too. You've hardly left my side since you got back. I think getting out of this house would do you good."

Olivia handed her mother a small glass of milk. "No, this is where I want to be."

"I really think you should go. When does he want to go hiking?"

"It doesn't matter, Mom. I'm not going anywhere."

One hundred and sixty miles to the north, Russo's Tavern occupied a corner of the third block of the small main street of Ontonagon, Michigan for seventy-three years. With a steadily declining population—currently at 1,308—, the bar depended on visitors to the huge Porcupine Mountain Wilderness State Park to stay open.

The front door opened. Bartender Paul Karppenin turned to see who had come in. He smiled. "Hey, Charlie. I was just thinking about you."

Charlie sat down at the long bar. "Oh?"

"Well, I guess I was really thinking about me first and then you. I was wondering if you heard anything about my application."

Charlie shook his head as Paul set a tall mug of beer in front of him. "No, we've got a hiring freeze going on from Washington. Not sure how long that's going to be in effect."

Paul frowned. "Damn. I need to find a job. It would be great if I could work for the park. I'd be outside most of the time. It would be nice to get back into the woods."

"How's your degree coming?"

"Ah, kind of slow. I'm taking a few classes online, but I don't think I'll have my bachelor's degree for another year and a half."

Charlie took a sip of beer. "That may be a problem. They're really pushing for a four-year degree now." He smiled. "You want to get back to the woods. Once I got my master's, they stuck me behind a desk. I get to drive around every now and then, but most of the time I'm pushing a pencil. Are they still closing this place?"

"As far as I know. Tearing the whole building down and putting up a car wash."

Charlie shook his head. "A car wash. I can't believe it. How'd they ever push that through the planning commission?"

Paul smiled. "When Fred Mattson speaks, everyone listens."

"Yep. Money and power. They go hand in hand. It's a shame this old building's going to have to go." He looked around the bar. "It's got so much character."

"To say nothing about putting us all out of work. Anyway, enough of that. When are they going to reopen the Summit Peak Trail?"

"It reopened last week. We didn't want to make a big deal of it, so we kept it kind of low-keyed."

"That poor hiker. I bet he doesn't get lost from now on."

"Yeah. He spent a long night up on the Summit Peak Trail." Charlie leaned forward and lowered his voice. "That's what I came in here to tell you, but you can't mention it to anybody. It hasn't made the news yet."

Paul stepped closer. Why had Charlie lowered his voice? There were only three other customers in the bar. Two of them were sitting at a table near the entrance. The other guy, Duck Lindquist, was sitting by himself at the far end of the bar. Paul asked, "What's going on?"

"Did I tell you that at first when they found the guy, they thought he was all upset about having to spend all night in the woods? But when they finally got him calmed down, that wasn't it at all. He led them to a spot off the trail where he'd found that skull."

"No. I never heard all the particulars."

"Well, tomorrow we're having a meeting up at headquarters. We're getting a briefing from the coroner and forensic anthropologist."

"How long has it been since they found the skull?"

11

Charlie thought. "Five or six weeks, I think."

Paul grabbed a glass and poured himself a soda. "I wonder what they figured out. That should be interesting."

Chapter 3

BEING CAREFUL WHERE he grabbed them, Arnold Spivey pulled sheets off the bed from the upstairs bedroom. He was wearing a pair of yellow plastic gloves, but he still didn't want to touch the mess. Why was it everyone thought they had to rut around like animals just because they were on vacation?

A large gray cat jumped on the bed. "Get off there, Daisy!" When he reached for the cat, it leaped to the floor. "You're not supposed to be up here. It's for our guests."

It had been his idea to advertise two of their bedrooms on the Internet. Money was tight when his father had taken off. Their old farmhouse always seemed to be needing some kind of expensive repair. Being so close to Lake Superior, with the constant wind, heavy winter snows, and the wide seasonal temperature changes took a heavy toll on the old structure.

Because they were so close to the Porcupine Mountains Wilderness Area, Arnold hoped the two rooms he and his mother offered would attract hikers in the summer and cross-country skiers in the winter. They had. But he hadn't really thought everything through before he posted their rooms for rent online eight months before.

Having strangers in the house and putting up with their messes, like this disgusting bed sheet, wasn't what he'd

13

envisioned. Mother's botched operation hadn't been in the plan either. Now the wheelchair she was confined to kept her on the first floor. She was still able to cook the advertised breakfast, but that was about all she could handle.

He stripped the bed in the other room, peeled off his gloves, and was about to carry the laundry basket downstairs, when he paused. He pulled out a handkerchief and stood on his tip-toes so he could reach a large, round clock that was mounted on the wall. He wiped a thin layer of dust from the glass face and then stepped back. The view from the hidden camera built into the clock would now be perfect. He grabbed the laundry basket and carefully navigated down the steep, narrow staircase.

His mother met him in the foyer. "Watch out, Arnold. You're going to step on that sheet. Can't you put them in the basket so they don't drag on the stairs?"

He set the basket down and grabbed the long end of the trailing fabric. He felt something cold and wet against his fingers. He jerked his hand back, ran over to the kitchen sink, and pumped soap out of a dispenser. "Dammit, Mother!"

She wheeled herself near the doorway. "What's the matter?"

"You made me stick my hand into…a mess."

She spun her chair around and laughed. "Oh. It's not going to kill you. I'm sure you've handled much worse when you're all by yourself down there in your room in the basement."

A hot blush crept up around his neck as he continued to scrub his fingers. Not bothering to comment, he wiped his hands, grabbed the basket, and stomped down the basement steps.

Once in the laundry room, he stared at the basket. Dammit. He had left his gloves up on the second floor. He flipped open the lid of the washer, turned the basket upside down, and shook it vigorously. No way was he going to touch those filthy sheets again.

Olivia Thompson was in her room struggling to understand a pre-calculus problem from a book she had brought home to study over the summer. Her cellphone rang. She glanced at it, smiled, and answered, "Hello, Tommy."

"I've been thinking about this hiking trip. It's not going to be any fun without you. I have to go right by your place on my way up there. Why don't you come with me?"

She sighed. "How many times do I have to go over this with you? I don't want to leave my mother. She's very sick. I'm busy doing a lot of things around here. I was hoping my sister would pitch in, but that's not happening."

"I bet she'd have to pitch in if you weren't there. Like gone hiking with me. It's only for a few days, Olivia. It's not like we'd be gone two weeks or anything."

"That wouldn't matter. My sister still wouldn't help. She's something else. But I have to say, Mom looks better today than she has since I've been home. She actually ate most of her lunch. I was really surprised. And...she wouldn't stop asking questions about you."

"I hope you told her how handsome I am."

Olivia laughed. "How could I not. She actually wants me to go hiking with you." There was a long silence.

"She does? Then why aren't you going?"

"Like I told you, she's sick. She needs me to be here so she can rest."

"Maybe I'll just show up on your doorstep and talk to your mother myself."

"It wouldn't matter. I'd love to go. Really I would. But it's just not possible."

Duck Lindquist walked into Russo's Tavern and took a seat at the bar. "Hey, Paul, draft Bud, like always." He spun his barstool around and stared at a group of pretty girls. "Holy wah! Look at those beauties. They gotta be from downstate."

Paul finished drying a glass. "They are, Duck. They're collage girls from Michigan State. They're camping over at Three Rivers. The blonde who just stood up is Alexis. I tried to get a date with her for later tonight."

"Tried?"

"Yeah. I've been bringing them drinks for the last two hours. She walked over and asked about hiking trails. I told her about the Little Carp Trail, the Cross, and South Mirror, and then I tried to get her to go out with me. She said she already had a boyfriend."

"What about the other ones? Are they all tied up too?"

Paul washed another glass. "I don't know. Why don't you go find out?"

"Maybe I will. Hey, what ever happened to that old girlfriend of yours? She kind of looked like that pretty blonde over there."

Paul set the glass down. "Grace? You're right. She does look like her. We broke up almost a year ago. She moved to Chicago a few months later. Wanted me to go with her." He paused. "Can you see me living in Chicago?"

Duck pulled his wallet out and slapped a five-dollar bill on the bar. "No, just like I couldn't see myself working in Milwaukee last year. I've been back for three months now, and

I'm glad I am. I'll take another beer, and get yourself one on me."

Paul handed him a beer. "Here you go." He held up his glass of soda. "I quit drinking after Grace and I split up. Here's to you."

"Her old man owns all those car lots, doesn't he? Mattson Motors?"

"Yeah. I think he's got about seven of them now. And, he owns this building..." Paul paused. "That's soon to be torn down."

"That car wash thing really got passed?"

"It did. You're going to have to find another bar to drink in, Duck. This building's supposed to be torn down by the end of October."

Duck shook his head. "I can't believe they approved that. I thought this was some kind of historical building that couldn't be messed with?"

"So did we. But money talks."

"You should've hung on to her. You'd probably be running one of his car lots by now. Be making the big bucks."

Paul smiled. "No thanks. I don't ever see me working for any future father-in-law. I'm not the best at taking orders."

Duck laughed. "Me either. So you quit drinking, did you?
"I did."

"I wondered about that. I've been coming in here ever since I got back from Milwaukee, and I've never seen you have a drink."

"Things kind of got out of hand. I was drinking way too much, and Grace was putting me to shame. After she left, I thought 'who needs it.'" He rang up Duck's money. "Anyway, what are you doing for work since you got back? There aren't many jobs around here."

"I know. I'm lucky. I can work for myself. I learned the jewelry business in Milwaukee. I make my own stuff and sell it online. Every Wednesday I drive over to Fines Jewelry store in Houghton and clean and repair things their customers bring in."

"Yeah. You're lucky," Paul said. "It pays to have a trade. Especially around here." He stepped back and stared at Duck. "How'd you ever get that nickname, anyway? I don't think I ever heard your real name."

Duck took a sip. "My real name's Dennis. Dennis Lindquist. I don't think anybody around here knows my real first name. They've been calling me Duck since I was twelve. You never heard that story?"

"No, and I've often wondered about it."

"Well, like I said, when I was about twelve, a bunch of us guys were over at Stinky Johnson's house. Did you know him?"

Paul laughed. "Stinky Johnson? Never heard of him."

"He got killed a few years ago. Hit by a logging truck. Anyway, he had a pet crow named Smokey. Now the damn thing never flew. It just glided from branch to branch. We were all running through a field behind Stinky's house when his crow decided to follow us. He came swooping in low, and Stinky yelled out to duck. I didn't know what he said, so I turned around to ask him. When I did, the crow flew right into my face. His beak poked me in the eye. I had to go to the hospital. I ended up wearing a patch for two months."

Paul laughed. "I'm surprised they didn't start calling you Patch instead."

Duck nodded. "You're right."

Paul was about to ask him if he was going to talk to the girls, when they all stood up and headed for the door. "Looks like your ladies are getting away from you."

Duck turned. "Just as well. Them trolls think they're too good for us yoopers, anyway."

Charlie Loonsfoot returned to his office after the management briefing. He sat at his desk and reviewed his notes. The skull found by the lost hiker had been sent to the Michigan State Police Crime Lab in Marquette where it was then shipped to the crime lab in Lansing.

After a thorough examination by the coroner and two forensic anthropologists, based on the size and thickness of the skull, the condition of the temporal line, the features of the lower sections of both orbits, and the absence of ridging on the Superciliary arch, it was determined that the skull had come from a female.

Charlie got up and refilled his cup with coffee. A young woman. What a damn shame. He glanced back down at the report.

The presence of a third molar and the amount of closure of the cranium sutures indicated to the investigators that the age of the skull was between seventeen and twenty-five years old. There was no chance that it had been associated with some kind of ancient Indian burial.

With no reports of a missing girl from the area, the determination was made to attempt to reconstruct the facial features before putting any information out to the media.

Chapter 4

OLIVIA TURNED TO Tommy. "I don't have real hiking boots. I hope these tennis shoes will be okay."

He glanced down at her feet. "They should be. It's only the Porkies. It's not like we're going to Glacier National Park or something." He returned his gaze to the road. "I can't believe you're here with me. What changed your mind?"

"It was Mom. She insisted I go."

Tommy smiled. "She did?"

"Yes, I was spending a lot of time with her. And then she started to feel a little better. Our neighbor came over. She's been watching over Mother too. She agreed with her and said I should go. So here we are."

"That's great. Just great. We're going to have such a good time."

Olivia asked, "Are they called the Porcupine Mountains because we're going to see a lot of porcupines?"

Tommy shrugged. "I don't know. Maybe."

Gladys Spivey pushed her wheelchair to the doorway that led down to the basement. "Arnold, what are you doing down there?"

Her son stopped hammering. "Nothing."

"You're making quite a racket for doing nothing."

He looked at his watch. It was time to go to town. He set his hammer down, grabbed his shopping list, and climbed up the stairs. Mother was waiting when he got to the top.

"I need you to come in the kitchen and reach the canister of flour for me."

He glanced at his watch again. "Ma, I gotta get downtown and pick up the list of things we worked on last night."

"You got plenty of time. It's only ten after eleven."

No, he didn't have plenty of time, but there was no way he was going to try to explain that to her. He followed her into the kitchen. "Where's the flour?"

She pointed to a cabinet above the sink.

He pulled the container down. "Anything else?"

She grabbed a recipe and read the ingredients. "Oh, I need the baking powder too." She pointed to another cabinet.

He rummaged through an assortment of spices and handed her the box. "Here." He turned toward the door. "I'll be back later."

She set the baking powder down on the counter. "I don't know what your hurry is. It's not like the stores are going to run out of anything we need on that list."

She grabbed an apron, leaned forward in her chair, and tied it around her waist. "You ran out of here last week around this time too. Like you had some kind of appointment or something."

He sighed. "This is when I like to get our weekly shopping done. Is that okay? Do I have to explain every little thing to you?"

She waved her hand. "Go. Get going if it's so darn important to you. But remember, we got guests coming at four o'clock."

Arnold wanted to slam the door behind him, but didn't. Yes, this trip to town was that important to him. In half an hour Leslie Babcock would be having lunch with her friend Kay Bloomfield at the Koffee Kup Kafe like they did every Tuesday. Two months before, after six weeks of trying, Arnold had figured out what Leslie's schedule was. He hadn't missed a lunch since.

He didn't actually have lunch every week. Sometimes he just walked by the diner's big plate glass window and glanced in. Other times he sat across the street where they couldn't see him watching. Today was going to be different. He was going to be sitting inside eating lunch before they arrived.

He drove his Chevy Blazer down the long, narrow road through the woods until he hit the main highway. He followed M-64 along the lakeshore for five miles, then crossed the river. He took a quick left on River Street which brought him to the restaurant. He scanned the cars parked in front of the café to make sure she wasn't already inside.

Arnold parked the car, stepped out, and took a few deep breaths. Maybe he should try to talk to her. He had only spoken to her twice. The last time was by accident three years before when he almost bumped her with his cart at the grocery store. He wasn't sure she even recognized him when he said he was sorry. But as he turned to continue shopping, she said, "That's okay, Arnold."

The first time they had spoken was in the seventh grade. He asked her to go to a dance the school was having. It had taken him weeks to work up the courage. He wanted to ask her over the phone rather than in person, but there was only one telephone in the house, and it was in the kitchen. His father always sat at the table after supper where he drank coffee, smoked, and read the paper. Even if there was a short window of opportunity when his dad stepped outside or went to the bathroom, Arnold didn't want to be in the middle of talking to her when his father returned.

Arnold walked up to the restaurant and peered inside. Good. She wasn't there yet.

He had finally worked up enough courage at school a few days before the dance. He tried to get her alone, but she was always surrounded by friends. Finally, he walked up and asked her. He knew his face was burning. That damn Molly Finster started to laugh. He never could stand her. Then she blurted out, "Hey, everyone. Arnold's asking Leslie to the dance."

He stood there waiting for Leslie to say something, but she just started laughing too. Finally, with the whole damn cafeteria staring at him, he turned and walked out to the hallway. He never attempted to speak to her again.

Arnold was in the middle of ordering a hamburger and fries when the door opened and Leslie and her friend stepped inside. They didn't notice him as the waitress guided them to a table on the other side of the room.

He pulled his shopping list from his pocket and pretended to study it. Every now and then he allowed himself a quick glance over in their direction.

As they took their seats, Kay Bloomfield leaned over and whispered, "He's here. He's sitting over there having lunch. I told you we'd see him today."

Leslie took a quick glance. "So what? Main Street's only five blocks long. How many restaurants do you think there are?

If Arnold's going to have lunch somewhere, chances are he'd be stopping here."

Kay leaned closer. "Leslie, come on. Almost every week we've met for lunch, we see this guy staring at us from one place or another. This can't be a coincidence."

Leslie picked up her menu. "Well, he must be staring at you because I don't think I've ever said one word to him."

"Me? I don't even know who he is. I never went to school here. I don't think he's following us around to gawk at me."

Leslie lowered the menu and glared at her. "Will you stop being so foolish and pick out what you want to eat?"

Arnold wished he could snap a picture of her with his phone, but he knew that would be too risky. Not that he didn't have any pictures of her. But today, with her wearing that pretty pink sweater, would have been something special. He turned in his chair and pretended to gaze out the window behind where they sat. He loved the fact that she didn't wear much makeup. Why should she? She was naturally beautiful. He liked the clothes she wore. No jeans and old sweatshirts for her. She looked like her clothes came from one of those fancy stores over in Marquette.

He turned as the waitress brought his meal. Why was that woman with Leslie always looking over in his direction?

He ate as slowly as he could. He didn't want this time to go by too quickly. Other than the supermarket incident, this was the closest he'd ever been to her since the seventh grade. He wished they had taken a closer table so he could smell her perfume.

Arnold glanced at them several times during his meal. Just as he was finishing up his last french fry, Leslie and her friend got up and walked over to the cash register. Should he say hello? Ask her how she was doing? His face started to blush. No, probably not.

Olivia stared out the windshield at the thick, impenetrable forest on both sides of the highway. She turned to Tommy. "I shouldn't be here."

"What?"

"I've been thinking about my mom. I never should have left." She put her hand on his shoulder. "Maybe we should turn around."

"Turn around? Are you crazy? I'm not turning around. Your mother practically begged me to take you."

"She was just feeling guilty. I know my sister isn't going to be any help, and our poor neighbor. She's going to be spending all her time over at our house."

Tommy kept his eyes on the road. "It's not like we're going to be gone two weeks or anything. We're coming back on Friday. Your mother would have a fit if I turned around and brought you back already."

Olivia fidgeted with her purse. "I suppose."

Twenty minutes later she said, "We haven't seen a car in over an hour. Where is this place, anyway?"

He smiled. "I told you it was in the middle of nowhere. I started coming here to hike a year before I joined the Marines. I thought if I was going to get in shape, this was the place to do it. It's great because it's a huge wilderness area, and you can find plenty of trails that aren't overrun with people."

She wrinkled her nose. "I think I'd like to have some people around if I'm going to be hiking in the wilderness. What about bears?"

"I'm sure there's plenty of them up here. But with so much land, they have lots of places to go and not bother

25

people. That's really not something you should be worrying about."

She gave him a half smile. No, she'd be worried about it. "Where are we staying? I know we're not camping. I made sure of that before we left."

"No, we're not camping. But I've done a lot of camping. It's fun. If I had known you were coming with me when I made the arrangements, I would have tried to find something a little nicer. But it should be okay. I found a place online. It's real close to the park, and it's not too expensive."

A look of panic crossed Olivia's face. "We don't have to share a bathroom, do we?"

Tommy thought for a moment. "Um, I can't remember. Oh, wait. There's only one, but the guy said we're the only guests staying there those days."

"Thank goodness."

He pulled out a paper with handwritten directions on it and handed it to her. "Here. We have to be close. Look for Turner Lane. It should be off to the right. They said it's on the lake."

Olivia reached into her purse and pulled out her cellphone. "Let me type in the address. My GPS will find it."

"I don't think that's going to help us much. I can't get any signal here, but you can try."

She looked at her phone and frowned. "No bars."

They drove another half mile, and then she pointed. "Slow down. There it is. Turner Lane."

Tommy hit the brakes and jerked the steering wheel. "This is a road? Looks more like a deer trail." He eased down a narrow dirt lane. In the distance, where the pine trees cleared, loomed an old farmhouse. The deep blue waters of Lake Superior sparkled behind it.

Olivia stared out the window. How had he found this place? Calling it dilapidated would be doing it a favor. She turned to him. "Really? This is where we're staying?"

He slowed the car. "Ah, wow. It…it didn't look this bad online."

Olivia continued to stare out the window. "We must be on the wrong road. This can't possibly be the place."

"It said Turner Lane where we turned, didn't it?" Have you seen any other houses? The road ends right up there. That has to be the house."

She turned to him. "I…I don't think we should stay here."

Tommy pulled up closer and parked the car. "Look, we're going to be hiking in the mountains most of the time. Let's see what the place looks like inside."

"Okay, but the room has to be clean. I'm checking the sheets and towels first thing."

Tommy nodded. "Sure. Hey, what time is it?"

"Three-thirty."

"Shit!"

"What?"

"The instructions said check-in was at four o'clock. It sounded like they were pretty strict about that."

"We could sit in the car for a while," Olivia suggested. "Or, I know. Why don't we walk behind the house so we can see more of the lake?"

Tommy glanced at the house. "I'd like to be able to get our things unpacked. But okay. Let's go."

Arnold was busy in the back of the basement when his mother called. "Arnold, the guests have arrived."

27

He put his glue gun down. "Okay, I'll be right up." He picked up several large pieces of foam board, stashed them in the coal bin, and shut the door. He climbed the stairs and found her sitting in her wheelchair at the kitchen table.

"Where are they?"

"They sat in the car for a few minutes and then went back by the old barn."

"Dammit! Didn't they see the sign? It's not safe to be walking around back there." He grabbed a hat from a hook on the back door and stepped outside.

"Looks like there's a hole in the roof," Olivia said as they passed an old barn.

"Yeah. Don't sneeze. I think the whole building would collapse if you did. And that garage. Had it ever seen a coat of paint? "

She pulled out her phone and took a picture. "I love the look of dilapidated buildings. So much charm." She made her way over to a weathered split rail fence that ran along a steep drop-off. "Tommy, come see."

He turned away from the barn and joined her. "Nice. Look at those whitecaps." He leaned closer to the fence. "Sure is a long way down to the shoreline."

Olivia snapped another picture. "I've got to share this on Facebook." She shivered and leaned closer to him. "The wind off the lake is freezing. Sure doesn't feel like July."

"They say it's the deepest of the Great Lakes. I guess it never warms up."

She stared at her phone. "The picture won't send. I'm not getting a connection."

A door slammed. They both turned as an overweight man in his late twenties approached them. He had on a pair of grimy jeans and a red plaid, flannel shirt. A Detroit Tigers cap rested precariously on his head over a thick clump of straw-colored hair.

"Looks like we've got some company," she whispered to Tommy.

"Are you Thomas Riggins?"

Tommy extended his hand. "I am. You must be Mr. Spivey."

Arnold ignored Tommy's attempt at a handshake. "Come on. Let's check you in. You're not supposed to be back here. Did you see the sign?"

Tommy glanced behind him. "Sign? No, sorry. We didn't see any sign."

Arnold pointed toward their car. "It's over there. This barn's about ready to fall over. We've had people almost slip off the cliff. It's all sand, but it goes down about six hundred feet. Insurance company says we can't have people back here." He turned and started walking back to the house.

As they got near the car, Tommy popped open the trunk and grabbed their bags. They followed Arnold up a set of worn steps.

"Watch out for those boards." Arnold pointed to a section of the porch. "They're kind of rotten."

As they neared the house, a shrill ringing noise sounded. Olivia jumped. "What's that?"

"It's an exterior ringer for the phone. I need to hear it when I'm outside, now that we got people staying here. Ma doesn't want to be bothered."

Once inside the living room, Arnold went over to an old desk and picked up some papers. He glanced at them and then looked at Olivia. "You got another guest? I don't see her listed here."

"Ah, oh yes. She decided to come with me at the last minute."

Arnold tapped the papers with his index finger. "That'll be another fifteen dollars."

Tommy pulled out his wallet. "Here you go."

"Thanks." Arnold stuffed the bills into his shirt pocket and pointed to a narrow staircase. "Your room's up there. Number Two."

Tommy picked up the suitcases. "We're going to do some hiking in the Porkies. Do you have a favorite trail we should check out?"

Arnold shook his head. "I'm not much of a hiker. The entrance to the park's two miles away. Turn right when you pull onto the highway. There's a key to the front door on a table in your room." He turned away and then stopped. "Oh, my mother's health isn't the greatest. She turns in pretty early. If you come home late, try to be quiet."

Olivia followed Tommy up the stairs to their room.

Once inside, he walked over to a window and peered out. "We got a great view of the lake." He surveyed the room. "It's not fancy. But I think it will work."

She ran her finger over the windowsill and collected a ball of dust. "Yeah. It's not fancy." She pulled back the covers and inspected the sheets. "They look clean."

Tommy breathed a sigh of relief. "Well, it is what it is. Like I said, we're not going to be here most of the time anyway."

Olivia pointed. "Look, there's a pretty cat sitting in the corner."

Tommy stepped back. "Get the damn thing out of here. I'm allergic. I'll be sneezing all night."

She went over and petted it. It looked up and began to purr.

"Out, out. Get it out of here."

She gave it a gentle shove toward the door. "Shoo. Go back downstairs."

Tommy stepped into the hallway. "Come on. Let's drive over to the park. We can unpack later."

Back in the basement, Arnold stepped into the coal bin. There hadn't been any coal for about sixty years. The floor was cement, but clean. Three of the walls were finished. He patched together many small pieces of thick foam and rolls of insulation. He crossed his arms and looked around. One more wall and the room would be completely soundproofed.

Twenty-two pictures of Leslie Babcock adorned one of the walls. Four pictures had been clipped out of his yearbooks. Freshman year through senior. The rest of the photographs were ones he'd been able to snap during the last few months. Mother threw a fit when he bought that new color printer. She didn't think they needed one. He smiled. They needed one, all right.

He pulled on one of the chains that were bolted to the wall. It wasn't going anywhere. His father had been a pack rat. Almost everything he needed had been somewhere in the old barn. What he couldn't find, he was able to purchase online. He picked up a package of zip ties. Good old Amazon sold everything.

He turned to the wall where the door was. It was the last one he needed to insulate. It shouldn't take long. He had the materials. If he wasn't disturbed, he might be able to finish it today. Then he'd have the perfect soundproof room hidden behind a mountain of junk at the back of the basement. A place where his mother's wheelchair could not get to, and a place where those filthy, sheet-staining guests would never venture into.

He gently removed a picture of Leslie from the wall and stared at it. Things would be different. The picture fluttered to the floor as he picked up a two-foot section of insulation and carefully fitted it to the wall.

Chapter 5

"SHE'S WHERE?" RACHEL Thompson asked, glaring at her mother.

Joyce picked up her cup of tea. "She went hiking up in the Porcupine Mountains with a friend of hers."

"Hiking? The Porcupine Mountains?" Rachel stood with her mouth open.

"That's what I told you, dear."

"Mother, this is absolutely ridiculous. First of all, Olivia doesn't hike. And then there's the fact that she can't stand to have a bug anywhere near her. Where did she come up with a story about going hiking in the mountains?"

Joyce sipped her tea. "Probably from the nice gentleman who picked her up."

Rachel's arms flew into the air. "She went with some guy? My sister?"

"Oh, for goodness sake. Stop being so dramatic and sit down. What's wrong with Olivia having another boyfriend?" She paused. "You've certainly had your share."

Rachel rubbed her forehead. "Oh, please. Not this lecture again."

"She didn't want to go, but I made her. She wanted to stay here and hover over me. I told her if I needed anything, I'd give you a call."

"What about Elaine?"

Her mother stared at her. "Why should Elaine be bothered when I have a very capable daughter across town?"

Rachel smiled.

Joyce continued, "Anyway, I think it's wonderful Olivia's seeing someone. I swear, sometimes I thought she'd never get over Johnny's death."

Rachel grabbed her coffee cup. "He should have never joined the Army. I don't know what he was thinking."

"He wanted to serve his country. And we know there's no work around here. They could have had a wonderful life together if…if that hadn't happened."

"You think so? I don't think they were a good match. He wasn't always nice to her."

"What do you mean?"

"He had a temper. He yelled at her a lot." Rachel paused. "Kind of like Dad."

Her mother ignored her last statement. "Speaking of boyfriends, how's Jack?"

Rachel sighed. "That would be ex-boyfriend. He's back in jail."

"Oh, lordy. What this time?"

"I really don't want to talk about it, Mother." She stood up. "I better get going."

"Going? You just got here."

Rachel leaned over and kissed her mother's forehead. "I'll see you later."

A slap on the back startled Paul. He turned to see Charlie Loonsfoot standing behind him.

"What are you doing drinking at a competitor's place?" Charlie asked.

"Join me," Paul said, pointing to the stool next to him. "New scenery. I'm checking out the competition. These guys come in and see us all the time. We frequent their establishment too. Duck and I walked over together. I like it here. Sudsy's is a great place."

Duck rotated on his bar stool. "Hi, Charlie."

Charlie sat down next to Paul. "I'm just giving you a hard time." He turned to the bartender. "I'll have a Porcupine Ale."

Paul asked, "How's your promotion going?"

Duck leaned over. "You got a new promotion?"

Before Charlie could answer, Paul said, "He sure did. Once he got that master's degree, he landed a cushy management job."

Duck smiled. "Looks like the drinks are on Charlie."

"So how's things up at the park?" Paul asked.

"We're doing okay, but this rainy summer's keeping the numbers down. Not good for the budget, but what can we do? We can't control Mother Nature now, can we?"

"Yeah, we're feeling it too. At least it was nice out today."

Duck jumped off his bar stool. "Guys, you're not going to believe this. I got a call from that jewelry store in Marquette where I repair things. They said somebody from the Haverhill mansion was asking for a jewelry repairman, and the store recommended me. Yesterday they called me. I'm going to be doing some work over there Saturday morning."

Charlie let out a low whistle. "The Haverhill mansion? I thought that place was abandoned after the war."

"I thought so too," Duck said. "But I guess an old woman, the daughter of old Mr. Haverhill, still comes there for a few months every summer. I was shocked when I got the call."

Paul's eyes widened. "Wow! I've never met anyone who ever set foot in that place. When you get over there, you gotta tell us what it looks like. Do they still own the old Portage mine?"

"What's to own?" Duck asked. "They closed it down in the fifties because it was too expensive to get the copper out that was still down there. I'm sure it's full of water by now."

Paul smiled. "Looks like you got a lot of questions to ask when you get there."

Olivia limped as she exited the trail and headed toward the car. Beside her, Tommy stomped along, a frown on his face. When she'd asked him to stop, he turned around with a look she had never seen before. His attitude seemed to soften, at least a little, when she showed him the huge blister on the heel of her left foot, but he had given her the silent treatment all the way back to the car.

"I'm sorry, Tommy. I guess these shoes aren't the best for hiking. I wish we could have started on a trail that wasn't so steep."

He whirled around. "Ah, did you forget we're in the Porcupine *Mountains*? The mountains. Not the Porcupine hills or…prairie."

She stepped away from the car and stared at him. He had never talked to her like that before. A tear ran down her cheek. She turned away.

He walked over and put his arm around her. "I'm sorry. I just wanted you to see the vista at the top of the mountain.

It's magnificent. I hiked up there last year with my brother, and I wanted to come back and see it again."

She wiped her face. "Maybe you should have taken your brother with you instead of begging me to come. You should have known I wouldn't be able to keep up with you. I told you I wasn't a hiker."

"I know. I know. You're right. What was I thinking? Sorry. Get in the car. Let's go get something to eat. I'm starving."

She climbed into the car but sat as close to the passenger door as possible. It was a quiet ride into town as she concentrated on the view out her window. When they entered the city limits, her phone beeped and pinged.

"What the hell's that?" Tommy asked.

"I must have a connection to the Internet. My e-mails and pictures must have gone through."

Tommy pulled up in front of a dilapidated building that needed a fresh coat of paint. "I need a drink." He jumped out of the car and waited for her near the door.

She followed him into Sudsy's where they took seats at the bar. She ordered a glass of red wine. Tommy ordered a double whiskey and water.

The bartender set their drinks down in front of them. "You folks visiting the area?"

"Yep," Tommy grunted.

Olivia nodded. "Yes, we're hiking in the park. It's so beautiful. We only walked one trail. It was kind of steep." She looked down at her foot. "It gave me a big blister."

"Hold on a minute." The bartender rummaged through a drawer and then spread out a state park map. "Here. Take a look at this." He pointed to a spot on the map. "You see this trail?"

Olivia looked to where he was pointing. "Yes."

Tommy stared out the window.

"It's the Union Spring Trail. It's a good one to start out on. It meanders through a nice forested area. Not too steep, and it ends up at a pretty lake. I've seen deer there. One time I saw a moose munching on some lily pads way out in the water."

Olivia smiled. "I'd love to see a moose." She turned to Tommy.

He had swiveled around on his stool and was staring in the opposite direction.

"You might want to stop over at Lakeside Drugs. They've got some pads you can put on your heels. You don't want that blister to break and get infected."

"Thank you. I'll do that."

The bartender turned the map around. "Another nice trail is—"

Tommy downed his drink, pulled out his wallet, and slammed a ten-dollar bill on the bar. He grabbed Olivia by the arm and pulled her off her seat. "Come on. We're outta here."

Olivia yelled, "Tommy! You're hurting me!"

He continued to drag her toward the door.

She tried to pull away. "What are you doing?"

"I don't need some asshole coming on to you. And you, batting those eyelashes at him like you never saw a man before."

Seated at the bar, Charlie turned to Paul. "Hey. Something's going on over there."

"What the hell's he doing?" Paul jumped up and ran over. "Hey, buddy. Get your hands off her."

Tommy turned and glared. He kept his grip on Olivia's arm. "Watch out, hayseed. I'm a Marine, and I'll mop the floor with you if you don't get the hell out of my way."

Paul grabbed Tommy's forearm. "Let go of her. I was in the Marines myself, my friend. You want to step outside and do this man to man, let's go. But you don't need to be manhandling a woman to try and show everyone what a big shot you think you are."

Tommy released his grip on Olivia and pointed to the door. "Get in the car." He turned back to Paul. "I'll let it go this time. But you tell that bartender he'd better be careful who he puts the make on next time."

Olivia stopped in front of the door and rubbed her arm. "Tommy, come on. Let's go."

He brushed past her and stepped out into the parking lot. "I should teach that big hick to mind his own business."

Paul stood with his arms crossed and watched as they traversed the parking lot.

Olivia's arm was throbbing. "What…what's wrong with you? You hurt me back there."

He stopped in front of the car. "Are you stupid or something? Can't you figure out when some creep is coming on to you? All that sweet talk about the trail and the bandage and everything. And you're just sitting there hanging on that guy's every word."

"What are you talking about? He wasn't coming on to me. I'm sure he talks to hikers every day. He probably knows all the trails around here. He was just being nice."

Tommy jerked open the car door. "Think what you like."

They drove in silence for a few blocks before he pulled into a parking lot. "Come on. Let's get something to eat."

Olivia preferred to sit in the car by herself, but all that walking and fresh air had made her hungry too. Reluctantly she got out of the car and followed him into the restaurant.

A waitress showed them to a booth, but instead of sitting across from her, Tommy slid in next to her. He tried to take her hand, but she pulled it away. "Look. I know you're mad about what happened. But I had a girlfriend once who got picked up at a bar by some jerk bartender just like that guy. You don't think he was trying to come on to you, and I guess you can have that opinion. Maybe I kind of jumped to conclusions because of what happened with Susan. I'm sorry." He sat so close to her, he jammed her into the corner. His body heat radiated against her.

"I still think the man was just trying to be nice to us." She tried to push him away, but he didn't move. "Tommy, you hurt me. I can't believe you grabbed me like that and dragged me across the floor. Everyone was looking at us. Then when that man came to help me, I thought you were going to cause a big fight right in front of everybody."

"I'm sorry I grabbed you. You're right. That should never have happened. Let's try and get over this. We've got a few more days up here. I want you to have a good time. I know your foot hurts. Maybe tomorrow we should check out the trail that guy told us about. That easy one. What do you say? Would you like that?"

She stared at the table. What would she like? To be back home with her mother. That's what she'd like.

Chapter 6

ARNOLD SAT AT small desk in his basement room. He was glad he had moved his bedroom down there. First off, he didn't want to be that close to the guests staying in the room next to his. By moving his room to the basement, they were now able to rent out two rooms instead of one. He had plans for some of that extra income.

It had been a good decision, because now he was able to monitor both rooms with his hidden cameras, and he never had to worry about someone busting in on him. It also put him much closer to the special room he'd been constructing.

Upstairs the front door opened. Arnold cocked his head. It had to be that new couple in Room Two. He grabbed a remote and turned on his monitor. They entered their room. Something seemed off. They weren't talking. The girl grabbed a paperback, plopped down in a chair across the room, and started reading. The man walked over to a small desk by the window and made himself a drink. He stared out over the lake.

What had happened? The last time he watched them, there had been a lot more interesting action. It didn't look like he'd get a replay tonight.

41

After ten minutes, she was still reading, and he continued to gaze out the window. Arnold switched off the screen and went over to two locked trunks positioned at the end of his bed. He pulled a key from his pocket, bent down, and opened the smaller one.

Unlike the other chest, which was filled to the top, this one was less than a quarter full. He reached in and ran his fingers through an assortment of panties and bras. Each provided a memory of one of his guests.

Arnold's rule was to take only one item. That is, if the guest was worthy. One item and one item only. That way, nothing would be missed. No suspicions would be raised, and no questions would be asked.

He gently closed the lid, locked the chest, and stared at the other trunk. He hated that box. That's where his *pretty* clothes were kept. The ones he was made to wear when he was a child.

"Arnold," his mother called from the kitchen.

He jumped. "Yes?"

"I need you up here."

He climbed the stairs to the kitchen. "What is it?"

She pointed to a high shelf. "The flour canister. You might as well bring me the sugar too."

He reached up, grabbed the containers, and set them on the counter. "Why don't you just keep them down here? You're constantly making pies for our guests, and you always need flour and sugar. Why do I constantly have to get them down for you? Wouldn't it make sense to just keep them on the counter where you can get to them?"

She moved her wheelchair next to him. "We've had this conversation before, haven't we? Let me think. Maybe thirty times? You know I don't like a cluttered countertop. For the life of me, is it really that hard for you to reach up there for me?" A cigarette bobbed up and down from the corner of her mouth as she spoke.

"You shouldn't be smoking in the house. We advertise this place as a smoke free environment."

"It's my house, and I'll smoke in it if I feel like it. You advertised this as smoke-free, not me."

He grabbed hold of a kitchen chair. How stupid could she be? "Ma, we have to do that to get traffic. You don't mind the money we've pulled in since I decided to rent out those rooms, do you. The money that's kept you out of some crappy rehab place, living with a bunch of strangers."

She pulled the cigarette from her mouth and knocked the ashes off into an ashtray that was clipped to her chair. "You sound more like your father every day. I keep wondering when you're going to get in that ratty car of yours and drive off into the sunset just like he did. Here one minute and gone the next. Abandoned his family. What a poor excuse of a man he was, and here you are sounding just like him."

Arnold clenched his teeth. Tears blurred his vision. He spun around and stomped down the stairs to the quiet, dim sanctuary of the basement.

Elaine ladled out a bowl of soup and set it down in front of Joyce.

Joyce struggled with her napkin. "Thank you. I'm so sorry I had to bother you again. I...I just don't know what's going on with Rachel. I can't depend on her like I can Olivia."

"Don't worry about it. Speaking of Olivia, how's her trip going? Have you heard from her?"

Joyce frowned. "She's only called once. She said her cellphone reception wasn't very good up there."

43

"Was she having a good time?"

"She was, I guess. I don't know. It wasn't anything she said, just the sound of her voice. I…I didn't get a great feeling that she was enjoying herself. I'll be glad when she gets home."

"I'm not surprised," Elaine said. "Olivia's not your rugged outdoor type."

Joyce nodded. "That's for sure."

Elaine took a sip of coffee. "At least she was able to get out of the house and see something different."

Chapter 7

OLIVIA RUBBED HER eyes and yawned. Sunlight spilled into the room creating dancing shadows as maple leaves blew in the wind. For a short time, she was confused about where she was. She looked over at the empty half of the queen-sized mattress and sat up. Had Tommy left?

She slipped out of bed and wrapped herself in a terry cloth bathrobe. Floorboards squeaked outside the bedroom door as a key slid into the lock. The door opened, and Tommy entered holding a large bouquet of flowers.

"Where did you get those?" Olivia asked, suddenly relaxed.

"I asked Mrs. Spivey. She told me about a farmers' market not far from here." He handed her a vase. "She gave me this so you'd have something to put them in."

"They're so beautiful."

"How's your foot?"

Olivia looked down. "Looks better than yesterday. If we pick up a couple of those bandages at the drug store, I'm sure I'll be able to do that easy trail."

"That's great. Let's grab some breakfast and try out that hike."

45

After picking up the bandages, they ate at a rustic log cabin restaurant on the way out of town and then stopped at the park's visitor center to confirm that the trail the bartender had told them about was suitable for a novice hiker.

Tommy pulled up to the trailhead.

Olivia glanced at the almost cloudless sky. "Looks like we have a nice day for our walk."

"We do." He exited the car and stood in front of a sign that displayed a map of the area along with a list of plants and animals they might see on the trail.

"Looks like there's two branches we could take." He moved his finger along the glass that covered the map. "The first one's a three-mile loop through several open fields. It says here there are a lot of wildflowers along this trail and a wooden walkway that goes over some swampy land." He pointed. "Let's do this loop first."

Olivia faced a light breeze. "Do you smell the pine? It's wonderful." She followed him to the trailhead.

"See these blue painted triangles?" Tommy asked. "That's what we have to follow."

The trail hugged a small stream for almost a mile and then took a sharp right where a big log served as a natural bridge over the water.

Tommy steadied Olivia as they carefully made their way over the rushing stream. Once on firm ground, he pointed out a beaver dam in the distance. After a few minutes of quiet observation, he whispered, "Look. There's two swimming over to the dam."

Olivia tried to take a picture with her cellphone, but the animals were too far away.

The trail eventually looped back to the starting place. Tommy suggested that they rest for a while and then hike the other fork of the trail.

The other branch had a slight incline that led through a magnificent old-growth forest of sugar maple, yellow birch, and eastern hemlock. Two miles into the second hike, they rested at a small lake.

"Just listen," Tommy said. "No sounds but the wind in the trees and birds singing."

Olivia sat on a fallen log. "It's so peaceful."

Tommy took two sandwiches out of his pack and handed one to her. "I'm not sure how good they are. But they were the best looking ones the convenience store had when we got gas."

"I'm sure they'll be fine."

Tommy suddenly spun around.

"What is it?" Olivia stood.

"I hear something." He pointed to the bushes and took a step back. "Something's in there."

Olivia grabbed his arm. Branches snapped, and the thick shrubbery in front of them swayed back and forth.

She pulled herself closer to Tommy. Whatever was in there was big, and it was heading in their direction. Just as they were about to run, an old man's head poked out of the underbrush. He let out a yelp and jumped back into the bushes. The leaves parted again, and he thrust his face out. "Sorry." He stepped out into the clearing. "Ya kind of scared me for a minute there. I wasn't expecting nobody."

Olivia peeked at him from behind Tommy. "Neither did we!"

Tattered brown corduroy pants hung on his small frame. His face was covered with a thick growth of gray whiskers, and his green-checked shirt was more patches than flannel. "Don't mind me." He spotted their lunch which Olivia had set out on a flat rock. "Um. You wouldn't have any of that to spare, would ya?"

Tommy glared at him as Olivia tossed him a big red apple.

"Here you go," she said as she picked up half a sandwich. "You can have this too if you want."

Tommy stepped forward. "Hey, wait a minute."

Olivia handed it to the man.

The old man grabbed it and shoved half of it into his mouth. He chewed for a minute and then wiped his lips on his shirt-sleeve. "Thanks. That's very kindly of ya." He gave a quick nod and then disappeared back into the forest.

Olivia turned to Tommy. "Did that really happen? Did we just see a living, breathing leprechaun or something?"

Tommy stared at the spot where the man had returned to the woods. "That was weird. They should really let us carry a gun up here. That guy looked like he's been living in some cave for the last ten years. He could have popped out of nowhere, cut our throats, and nobody would ever have known what happened."

Olivia shuddered. "Tommy! He seemed nice enough."

"He's probably hiding ten feet back there, ready to kill me for my wallet. Come on. We need to get the hell out of here."

Olivia packed up what was left of their lunch, and they started walking back to the trailhead.

Tommy picked up a thick stick and held it like a club. It seemed to take twice as long to get back to the car.

When they were safely inside the vehicle, Tommy locked the doors. "I'm driving over to the visitors' center. We got to tell them what happened."

She nodded. "Good idea."

When they got there, the woman at the counter was explaining some of the trails to another couple. Olivia and Tommy waited in the background. The woman finished up and motioned for them. "Can I help you?"

Tommy stepped forward. "Yes, I'd like to report something. My girl and I were walking the Union Spring Trail just now when some old lunatic jumped out from the bushes and scared the hell out of us."

Without any change in her expression or tone of voice, she asked, "What did this...lunatic look like?"

Olivia said, "He was a short, old man with white whiskers. He was wearing a flannel shirt that was all patched together."

The woman smiled. "Well, aren't you the lucky ones!"

"Lucky ones?" Tommy asked.

"Yes, you were fortunate enough to run into Prospector Pete. He's a legend around here."

Olivia looked at Tommy. "A legend?"

"He's been looking for gold up in the mountains for years. He's really not supposed to be doing it, but we can't get him to stop. We catch him every now and then and write him a ticket, but he goes right back. He's so elusive, some people don't think he really exists. They think we've made him up as some kind of publicity stunt. But now you know, he's no publicity stunt."

"Gold?" Tommy asked. "There's gold here?"

The woman nodded. "I'm not sure how much is here now, but during the late eighteen hundreds we had our own little gold rush. Marquette did too."

Tommy frowned. "I'm really surprised you let some goofy kook roam around the woods terrorizing hikers like that."

The lady folded her arms and stared at him. "You're telling me Pete terrorized you? We've never heard of him bothering anybody. Oh, he's asked people for food before, but never in a threatening manner." She cocked her head. "Exactly how did he terrorize you?"

Tommy grabbed Olivia's hand. "Come on, let's get out of here." As they approached the door, he turned toward the woman. "That old coot shouldn't be bothering anybody for sandwiches. Someone should hunt the creepy old fool down before he kills somebody."

Paul was happy to see that the bar was almost full. It was funny how quickly people responded to good weather. He set down Charlie Loonsfoot's second draft. "Did they ever find out any more about that skull on Summit Peak Trail?"

Charlie took a sip of the cold brew and wiped foam from his upper lip. "Yeah. They think it's from a young woman. Problem is, no girl's gone missing around here."

"How old do they think she was?"

"Late teens to late twenties."

Paul shook his head. "They can tell that from just the skull?"

Charlie shrugged. "I guess. Don't ask me how."

Paul pointed over to the front door. "Check this out. Look who just walked in."

Charlie didn't turn around. "Don't tell me it's my ex-wife."

"No, it's that guy who dragged his girlfriend out of Sudsy's last night."

"The Marine?" Charlie asked.

"Well, he called himself a Marine. He's walking over here. Wait until he notices us."

Tommy didn't see them. He found two empty stools about ten people down from Charlie. Tommy waited for Olivia to get seated and then sat down. "What do you want? A Merlot?"

She nodded.

When Tommy turned toward the bar to order, Paul was standing in front of him. Tommy gave a start. "Oh, you."

Paul smiled. "Yep. It's me. Just so you know, this is a nice, friendly place, and we don't put up with any trouble."

"What's that supposed to mean?" Tommy countered.

Olivia grabbed his arm. "Just order the drinks."

Tommy pulled away. "Give me a bottle of Stroh's and a glass of Merlot." When Paul left to get their drinks, Tommy turned to Olivia. "Did you see that guy trying to start something with me? 'We don't put up with any trouble.' He didn't have to throw that in my face. I'm just sitting here with you trying to get a damn drink."

"I'm sure he didn't mean anything by it." She tried to change the subject. "Can you believe that crazy old man we saw on the trail today? A gold prospector. I thought all of that had gone away a hundred years ago."

"I know. He looked just like one of those dusty old miners I used to see on reruns of *Gunsmoke* with my dad."

Olivia laughed. "He did. He really did."

Charlie waved Paul over. "Is that Duck sitting down there?"

Paul nodded. "Yeah. He's been here awhile. I'm about ready to shut him off."

Charlie threw a ten-dollar bill on the bar. "Tell him I'll buy him a beer if he comes down here and says hello."

"Okay. I'll tell him."

A few minutes later, Duck ambled over. "I hear you got a beer over here with my name on it."

"I do, Duck. I do. But here's what I want you to do first." Charlie pointed down the bar. "You see that pretty girl sitting next to the guy who looks like he's pissed off?"

Duck peered down the bar. "That pretty brunette?"

"Yeah. That's the one."

"What about her?"

"I want you to go over and cheer her up. Tell her she's pretty."

Duck smiled. "And then you'll buy me another beer?"

Charlie nodded.

"Okay."

"Hey!" Paul shouted from behind the bar. Both Charlie and Duck turned. "Don't listen to him, Duck. He's just trying to start trouble."

"Trouble? What trouble could there be in telling a woman she's pretty?"

"Just take my word for it." Paul turned to Charlie. "What the hell are you trying to do? Start World War Three? Tell you what. I'm going to get Duck a beer, and you're going to pay for it." Paul stared at him. "But he better not go over to that girl."

Charlie laughed. "Okay. I just thought it would be funny to see how her grumpy boyfriend would react."

Duck wandered back to his seat. He drained his glass and pushed himself away from the bar. A little unsteady as he stood up, Duck reached out and grabbed the guy sitting next to him.

"Get off me, Duck. Look at you. You need to get your ass home."

Duck smiled. "Not so fast. I'm gonna go get me a free beer."

"What are you talking about? There's no free beer."

Duck winked. "Watch me." He stumbled around the bar and slowly approached Tommy and Olivia. "Hey, man. I just got to tell you, you got yourself one hot woman." He swayed a few times and then almost collapsed against her. She jumped from the stool.

Tommy stood up. "You'd better get your drunk ass away from us."

Duck smiled. "No, I really mean it." He turned and stuck his face directly in front of Olivia. "She's real cute." He inhaled deeply. "And, oh…she sure does smell good too."

Just as Duck reached out to grab Olivia's arm, Paul noticed what was going on. He yelled, "Duck!"

"I told you to get lost," Tommy said, his voice getting louder. He grabbed Duck by the shoulder and swung him around. Tommy drew back, and his fist landed squarely on Duck's jaw.

Duck's head jerked back. He stumbled a few times, tried to catch his balance, collided with a bar stool, and collapsed onto the floor. The back of his head slammed hard against the old oak planks. He lay motionless. A small pool of blood puddled underneath his head.

The customer sitting next to Olivia crouched down next to him. "He's not moving. There's blood!" He looked up, eyes wide. "Is he dead?"

Tommy stepped back. "Dead?" He grabbed Olivia. "Come on. I gotta get out of here."

She pulled away. "No! We've got to help him." She snatched a handful of napkins and bent down to see where the blood was coming from.

Paul dialed 911 and ran out from behind the bar.

Charlie was leaning over Duck giving him chest compressions. After what seemed to be an eternity, Duck's eyes fluttered. He took a deep breath.

A woman pushed through the crowd. "Let me through. I'm a nurse." She knelt down and felt Duck's pulse, then looked up at Paul. "Get me a cold, wet towel."

Olivia stood up and looked around. "Tommy? Tommy?"

Chapter 8

RACHEL WATCHED AS a heavyset man in a dark charcoal suit glanced through her resume for the second time. He looked uncomfortable as he sat behind a small wooden desk. "We've gone over all the questions I had. Just one more thing."

"Yes?"

He leaned back, pulled off his glasses, and tapped them on the resume. "Our research shows you had a DUI a few years ago. Is that true?"

Rachel bit her lip. "Yes, but I went to all of the classes. I did my community service and got my license back."

"Any problems after that?"

"No, sir. Nothing."

He stood up and stuck out his hand. "Well, thank you so much for stopping by. We've got quite a few interviews to get through. We'll be making our selection in a week or two."

Rachel shook his hand and returned to the lobby. She let out a big sigh. She wouldn't be holding her breath for that job. It had gone just like the last seven interviews she'd been to during the last few months. That damn DUI.

Arnold walked outside to the back of the house. He hoped his mother was still taking a nap. He didn't need any of her incessant questions. He was holding a can of WD-40 lubricant spray. He reached down and pulled up a corner of the long, metal door that covered the old coal chute. The rusty hinges screeched as the door slowly opened. He covered them in a thick spray of oil and tried the door again. It operated smoothly and quietly. He smiled. Almost ready.

He returned to the basement and put the can away. One more test. He grabbed a large portable radio and set it in the middle of the modified coal bin. He switched the volume on to its maximum level, ran out, and slammed the door closed. Nothing. No noise escaped the heavy insulation. He went back inside and turned off the radio.

He pulled a key from his pocket and turned the dead bolt back and forth a few times. He locked the door and pulled on the handle. It didn't feel secure. He bent closer and examined it. The shaft of the lock looked short. Would it stand up to someone pushing from the other side? He yanked on the door again. Damn. Why had he bought the cheapest deadbolt at the hardware store? This wasn't going to work.

Half an hour later he mounted a long piece of two-by-four onto the door. The washers he had installed behind it made it pivot smoothly down into a U-shaped iron bracket he had bolted to the doorframe. He pushed the two–by-four into the bracket and pulled on the door. Much better. Nobody was going to kick their way out now.

He put away his tools and climbed the stairs to the kitchen. The door to his mother's bedroom was shut, but he could hear a muffled conversation. He put his ear closer to the door. Dammit! That pervert, Mr. Jacobson, must be visiting again.

Arnold's stomach tightened. He went to the foyer and peered out the window. Yes, Jacobson's truck was parked out front. This had been going on for almost three months now. Ever since Mr. Jacobson had separated from his wife. Every week, sometimes twice a week, he'd show up at their house. Then he and his mother would disappear into her bedroom. An hour later they'd come out looking like foolish eighth-graders. All giggles and red-faced. Sometimes Mr. Jacobson would sit and have a cup of coffee with his mother before he left.

Why did he let this bother him? It was nothing new. When his father was on the road driving truck, there was always a parade of men stopping by the house. The big surprise was that it continued after his mother was confined to that wheelchair.

Arnold glanced down at the credenza under the window. That damn picture. How many times had he lied to the guests about it? They wanted to know where the pretty little girl was. He wanted to scream as loud as he could that she was dead. Dead and gone, but he didn't. He always told them she was away at college. His pretty little sister was away at college. But it was all a big lie. The pretty little girl was him. He knew that someday someone was going to take a closer look and figure it out.

When he was born, his mother wanted a baby girl. She just knew it was going to be a girl. She had even picked out the name. Arlene. What a shock when her little girl showed up sporting a penis. Arlene turned into Arnold, but his mother's desire for a girl never went away. That's why there was a locker of pretty things at the end of his bed. It held the clothes and fancy wigs he'd been forced to wear until he went to junior high school. The trunk that he was forbidden to touch except when he had to haul it up to his mother's bedroom every now and then so she could rummage through it. This usually happened when she had had too much to drink. And having too much to drink seemed to be happening more and more lately.

A door opened and shut. Mr. Jacobson quickly walked to the foyer. He kept his head down, mumbled something incomprehensible, and brushed past Arnold. He descended the porch steps and headed toward his truck.

Arnold stood in the doorway. Maybe he should give Mr. Jacobson's wife a call and let her know what was going on. Why bother. They were separated. She probably didn't care.

He returned to the kitchen and cleared the dirty dishes from the table. He ran hot water and reached for a dishcloth.

His mother wheeled herself out of the bedroom. "Be careful with those plates. You already chipped one. What's your big hurry, anyway? You're running around the kitchen like there's no tomorrow."

"I've got someplace to go."

Gladys Spivey took off her glasses and polished the lenses with a napkin. "You've got somewhere to go? Ha. That's a good one."

Arnold gently put two plates away in the cupboard. "I'm visiting a friend."

His mother replaced her glasses. "A friend is it? I don't remember you having a friend since the tenth grade. Who's this mysterious person you've never mentioned until now?"

Arnold washed a coffee cup. "Just a friend. You don't need to be poking around every little nook and cranny of my life, you know. I can have a little privacy too. You don't tell me every time your friend Mr. Jacobson decides to pay you a visit, do you?"

Gladys smiled. "Oh, it's that kind of friend, is it?" Her smile disappeared. "You better not be going out to meet some bimbo you found on that Internet. I've seen what can happen with those deals. You think you're going over to some fourteen-year-old's house to get a little, and before you know it, ten cops run out from the bushes and arrest you."

Arnold threw the wet dishcloth into the sink. "I'm not meeting any fourteen-year-old."

His mother lit a cigarette and coughed. "Probably the only kind of girl that would have anything to do with you. Some idiot that's never kissed a boy before."

Arnold clenched his fists. He wanted to punch something. He grabbed his coat from the hook behind the back door and stomped down the back porch steps.

As he headed into town, Arnold glanced at the box that was sitting next to him in the passenger's seat. Thank goodness he had remembered to put it in the car that afternoon. Gloves, duct tape, and a big flashlight. It was the kind the cops used. Long and hefty.

He slowly drove through town and took care to obey all traffic signs. This was not the time to be tripped up by some minor infraction. He turned onto Airport Road. It was too early. He had been in such a hurry to get away from his mother, now he had to kill some time until it got dark.

He drove around town and stopped at Kiwanis Park. He watched several teenaged girls play volleyball until it got too dark. His heart beat faster. It was getting close. He pulled out of the park, turned down a side street, and pulled over. Leslie Babcock lived alone in a small clapboard house at the end of a long dead-end road. Where should he leave the car? He had driven by several times but had never been able to decide the best place.

After a few minutes, he threw the car into reverse and backed halfway down her street. That should work. Get her to the car and head out quickly. No need to turn around. He shut off the lights and killed the engine.

Flashlight in hand, Arnold pulled a bandana up over his face and started walking down her road. The night was cool. He looked up at the sky. A million stars blanketed the dark sky, and the moon was only a thin sliver. He hadn't thought about the moon. Good thing it wasn't full. He rounded a small curve, and there was Leslie's house. No strange cars were in the driveway. That was good. No need for unwanted visitors.

The flicker of a television lit up the living room. The window continually changed from bright to dark and back again. Where was she sitting? Was the back door open? He had snuck inside three weeks before when she had been at work. Her door had been unlocked that time.

Arnold stayed in the deep shadows of the woods. Just to be safe, he walked all the way around the garage before stepping onto the first step of the back porch. He positioned his feet as close to the sides of the old wooden steps as he could to keep the boards from creaking.

He snapped the flashlight off, stuck it in his back pocket, and grabbed the door handle. It turned effortlessly. The door swung open and he stepped inside. The hallway was dark.

He hugged the wall and inched his way to the kitchen. Only one tiny light from under the exhaust hood over the stove illuminated the room. He peered into the living room. Leslie's head and shoulders were silhouetted against the light from the television. She was sitting on the couch, facing away from him. He smiled. She was in a perfect position.

Arnold reached into his coat pocket and pulled out the roll of duct tape. As he was slowly peeling off a section, a low growl froze him in place. He glanced over his shoulder. A quick shadow moved down the dark hallway. The scrape of claws against the linoleum floor exploded in his ears. A dark shape raced toward him and then lunged. Huge teeth clamped down on his forearm. He struggled to remain upright.

A scream came from the living room. "Duke! Duke! What's going on?"

Arnold pulled the flashlight from his back pocket and slammed it down on the dog's head. Enraged, the dog bit down onto his arm even harder.

Arnold yelled out in pain as the dog shook its head from side to side. Arnold fell to his knees. He smashed the light against the dog's head again.

Finally, it let go. Arnold pushed himself up and stumbled down the hallway. He threw open the back door and ran for his car.

Screams came from the house. He tried to open the car door with his left hand, but his fingers refused to move. He pulled the door open with his other hand and jumped inside. The engine revved, and gravel sprayed as the car shot down the darkened road. He turned onto Airport Road and switched on his headlights.

He drove west onto Michigan Avenue and weaved along side streets until he was out of town. His arm was throbbing. A warm patch of blood soaked his pants where his arm had been resting.

Outside of town the road darkened as he left the city limits. He drove along the shore for several miles and then pulled the car over. He was about to pass out. He rolled down his window and breathed in the cool breeze from Lake

Superior. He felt as if he was going to be sick. He stuck his head out of the window. Two cars drove by, illuminating his vehicle with their headlights. He needed to get off the road. It was only three miles back to his house. He could make it.

As he drove down his long driveway, Arnold noticed another set of headlights had also turned off the main road. Another car was coming down his drive. Sweat broke out on his forehead. Had he been spotted? Discovered so quickly? He pulled up to the garage and turned off the car. He reached into his box and pulled out the hunting knife he had forgotten to take into Leslie's house. He slipped it under his belt and got out of the car. He ducked down behind a clump of trees along the driveway.

The car continued down the road and then came to a stop inches behind his vehicle. Arnold waited to see who would step out. His hand rested on the handle of the knife.

Arnold had a sudden impulse to flee into the woods. He tried to ignore his throbbing arm.

Both of the car's doors opened at once. Arnold crouched down against a tree. It was his renters. That pretty girl and her boyfriend.

"What do you mean you wanted to stay?" Tommy asked. "I told you, with my record I had to get the hell out of there."

"The man wasn't dead!" Olivia replied. "If you would have stayed inside and tried to help, you'd know that. I…I can't believe you just turned and ran outside."

"I got kicked out of the Marines for hurting a guy in a fight. I just got off probation for another fight. If they stick this on me, I'm looking to do some serious time. Like I said, we need to grab our stuff and get the hell out of here."

Olivia stopped. "I'm not leaving with you."

"What?"

"No, I'm not. What you did was wrong, and it sounds like this fighting thing is a pattern with you. I…I can't be with you anymore."

Tommy stared at her in disbelief. "Are you crazy? How are you going to get back home?"

Olivia thought for a moment. "I'll take a bus or have my sister come and get me. It doesn't matter. I'm not going with you."

He pushed her aside. "Suit yourself. I'm going to get my shit and get out of here."

Arnold remained hidden as Tommy walked to the house. Olivia stayed behind. She was only about twenty feet away. Arnold held his bleeding arm close to his body and tried not to make any noise.

After a few minutes, Tommy returned with his suitcase. "Are you sure you don't want to come with me?"

She nodded. "I'm sure."

He tossed her the room key and climbed into the car. As his tail-lights disappeared down the road, Olivia slowly walked toward the house.

Arnold waited a few minutes, enough time for her to get upstairs. He entered the house and went straight to the bathroom. He struggled out of his jacket. It took three attempts to get out of his blood-stained shirt. He stared down at several deep puncture wounds. No wonder his arm was killing him.

He grabbed a bottle of peroxide from the medicine cabinet and poured some onto his arm. He sat down on the toilet seat and tried not to scream as the peroxide bubbled around his wounds. He rinsed his arm off, patted it dry, and then wrapped several layers of gauze around his injuries. Arnold took a bottle of Advil and headed to his room.

Chapter 9

ARNOLD SAT ON the edge of the bed and rubbed his eyes. It was eight a.m. He hadn't gotten much sleep. His arm had throbbed all night, even after he had taken more Advil than he should have. He carefully unwrapped the bandage. His arm was red and swollen. Several spots of dark yellow had soaked through the bandage. He should get to the hospital. Would it be safe? The cops were probably waiting for someone to show up with severe dog bites. What kind of dog was that, anyway? Doberman? It must have been a Doberman.

The door flew open at the top of the basement stairs, and his mother yelled down for him. He closed his eyes. How was he going to hide this from her? If this made the local news, she'd be the first to put two and two together.

He yelled, "I'll be there in a few minutes." Why hadn't he taken the peroxide with him? He could have rinsed his arm off in the laundry tub. He grabbed a thick sweatshirt and slowly worked it over his head. It took several minutes before he could maneuver his injured arm into the sleeve. The slightest movement was enough to cover his face with a layer of sweat. He downed a few more pills and slowly walked up the stairs, cradling his injured arm. When he stepped into the kitchen, his mother glared at him. "What the hell happened to you?"

He went over to the counter and tried to pour a cup of coffee. His hand was shaking. "What do you mean?"

"Did you look at yourself this morning? You look like you've seen a ghost. You don't have a speck of color in you." She took a drag from her cigarette. "And you're walking all stiff-like. What the hell's wrong with your arm?"

"I…I banged it yesterday when I was trying to clean up the mess in the barn. A board fell down and … and smacked it real good."

His mother reached out. "Let me take a look at it. Is it broken?"

He jumped back. "No, it's not broken."

Olivia rolled over and peeked out from under the covers to make sure Tommy was gone. She had tossed and turned with terrible nightmares all night.

She bunched up the extra pillow behind her and let out a sigh. She didn't miss him. In fact, it was quite the opposite. After everything that happened, right from the beginning when he yelled at her for getting a blister on her foot, she was glad he was gone. She had been walking on egg-shells ever since they arrived. But she did need to find some way to get home.

What would be best? The bus? Was there a bus depot in the small town? Rachel? Olivia shook her head. Getting her involved would have to be a last resort. If there was a bus, what time did it leave? Certainly Mrs. Spivey or her son would know. She'd be happy to pay them to get her to the depot.

She looked at the clock on the other side of the room. She'd better get going.

Arnold's mother held a pair of metal tongs in her hand and stretched up from her wheelchair to peer at an iron skillet filled with frying bacon. "Did you hurt your arm during your date last night? Is that what happened? I bet some girl you met on that computer tried to fight you off."

"I didn't meet anyone on the computer, Mother."

"So what happened? Some father walk in on you and his fourteen-year-old daughter? Is that how you hurt your arm?"

Arnold's stomach tensed. He spun around. "Shut up!"

She pushed herself away from the stove and shook the tongs at him. "Don't you ever tell me to shut up. Not while you're living in my house, you don't. Do you understand?" She shoved the tops of the wheels on her chair, shot over to him, and grabbed his arm. "I'm telling you—"

Arnold yelled. As he pulled away from her, he crashed against the stove. The heavy skillet slid off the burner and overturned in his mother's lap. Sizzling grease shot up and splashed down the side of her face. She screamed.

Arnold grabbed the iron frying pan. "Look what you've done!"

She held her face and continued to scream.

The odor of her burned flesh hit him as his arm sent waves of pain shooting through his body. He lifted the heavy pan and swung it down against the side of her head.

She lurched sideways in her wheelchair and toppled onto the floor.

He started crying. "I hate you! I hate you!" He grabbed a large knife from a wooden block and bent over her. In a frenzy, he plunged the knife into her body again and again. Long sprays of blood flew up and splattered the walls. "Shut up! Shut up! Shut the hell up!"

Olivia shut her suitcase and listened. What was that noise? She stood up. Oh, no. Was there a fight downstairs?

Were they leaving? Afraid that she was about to miss her ride, she grabbed her suitcase and quickly descended the narrow stairway.

She set her luggage down and ran over to the open kitchen doorway. "Hello. I'm sorry to bother you, but—" She stepped back. What had she just seen?

She ran to the foyer and grabbed the door. It was locked. She whirled around as Arnold came running out of the kitchen. His shirt was covered in blood.

He grabbed her with a sticky, red hand and pulled her toward the kitchen. "Oh, no. You aren't going anywhere. Come on."

As they neared the doorway, she reached out and grasped the doorjamb. "No! I need to go home. Please. Let go of me!"

He gave her arm a sharp yank and pulled her away from the door. He dragged her through the kitchen and slowed to step around the overturned wheelchair.

His mother reached out for her and silently mouthed, "Help me."

At the top of the basement steps, he gave her a shove. "Down there."

She struggled not to lose her footing as he pushed her down the stairs. When they got to the bottom, he dragged her across the basement and stopped in front of a jumble of old trunks and clothes racks. He pushed through the assemblage and shoved her through a small doorway.

He slammed the door shut behind her, fished a key ring out of his pocket, and set the deadbolt in place. He pivoted the two-by-four down into the iron latch, leaned against the door, and tried to catch his breath.

Once the adrenaline rush from what had just happened was over, the pain from his puncture wounds swept over him. He closed his eyes, slid down to the floor, and started to shake.

What just happened? Mother was either dead or dying on the kitchen floor, and some girl he hardly knew was taking Leslie's place in the coal bin. Why did Leslie have to own such a vicious dog? His whole plan had been screwed up.

He sat there for over half an hour and then slowly stood up. He climbed back up the stairs and peered into the kitchen. The wheelchair was still on its side. Next to it, his mother lay still. There was blood everywhere. On the floor, the walls, and even on the ceiling.

He returned to the basement and grabbed a bucket and mop from the cleaning supply closet.

Back in the kitchen, Arnold put the bucket on the floor, leaned the mop against the refrigerator, and bent down near his mother's body. Her eyes were open. She wasn't breathing. He sat down on a kitchen chair and looked away. All the years of torment. Of dressing as a girl. The abuse. The scorn. The hatred that he wasn't her much-desired daughter was now gone. Done. Over.

The frying pan lay in a pool of blood. Maybe he should pick it up and frame it. Hang it on the wall. His liberating weapon. He put his head in his hands and tried to think. What to do now?

After a few minutes, he stood. There was a lot of cleaning to attend to. He folded up the wheelchair, wiped blood from its side, and shoved it into her room. He mopped the floor around her body several times with strong bleach water. It hadn't been easy using only his right arm. He had to stop to take more pills.

The cat walked in from the living room and slowly went over toward Mrs. Spivey's body. She lowered her head and sniffed at the pool of blood on the floor. The hair on its back stood up. It took a step backward and ran out of the room.

It was going to take a long time to clean this up, and it was all Leslie Babcock's fault. How was he to know she owned some kind of rabid dog? It could have been so easy. Wrap the tape around her mouth. Tie her up and throw her in the back seat. Cover her up with the blanket he had brought, open the coal chute doors, and slide her right into his newly prepared room. But no. Because of that damn dog, now some other girl-some stranger-was down in the room.

He spent the next three hours washing down the kitchen. Finally, his throbbing arm forced him to stop. He looked at the clock. It was a little after noon. He walked to the calendar on the refrigerator. Dammit! New guests were coming that afternoon. There was no way he was going to be able to get the house ready in time. Where was he going to hide his mother? She'd probably be okay in her room for a day or two, but what then? The barn? Maybe the barn. He couldn't be digging a grave out there with guests traipsing in and out. Arnold stepped into the foyer and pulled out the guest folder. He went back to the kitchen phone and hoped the number they had provided was a cell number.

A woman answered. Her voice was cheerful, but her demeanor changed quickly when he told her that they needed to make other plans. She wasn't very understanding. He hung up on her in the middle of her cursing rant. What kind of review would she be putting on the internet? Not a good one.

He returned to the kitchen, sat down, and eased his left arm onto his knee. The throbbing was getting intense. He tried to take his mind off it by making a pot of coffee. While he waited for it to brew, he found an old blanket and threw it over his mother.

As he poured himself a cup of coffee, the phone rang. Arnold checked the time. It was probably Mr. Jacobson calling. What was he going to tell him? That his mother wasn't going to be available for sex anymore because…because what? He killed her? Hardly. Arnold shook his head. Let it ring. He'd have to worry about that later when he wasn't so exhausted.

Joyce lifted her head from the pillow. "What time is it?"

Elaine glanced at a clock on the nightstand. "It's almost four-fifteen."

"They should be here by now. It only takes about three hours. I'm sure they'd have to check out of the room sometime in the morning. I thought she'd be home by now."

Elaine stood up and stretched. "Maybe they stopped at some of those tourist spots. They could have driven over to Munising and taken one of those scenic boat rides to the Pictured Rocks. Have you ever done that? It's a wonderful trip."

Joyce nodded. "Yes, I went up there with Al and the kids when they were young. I doubt Olivia even remembers." She reached for a glass of water. "She should have called if that's what they decided to do. It's not like her not to keep in touch. I swear, I've only spoken to her once the whole time she's been gone."

Olivia cradled her head and sobbed. How long had she been in here? It had to be hours. The room was dark. She had finally summoned up enough courage to crawl around on her hands and knees to try to figure out just where she'd been imprisoned. There was a mattress and a blanket. Some kind of chains hung from the wall. She found a roll of toilet paper next to a plastic pail. It had taken her eyes a while to become accustomed to the darkness. Only one very faint sliver of light entered near the ceiling at the far end of the room. It wasn't enough to illuminate much of anything. From her exploring she knew the room was tiny.

She closed her eyes and tried to erase from her mind the image of poor Mrs. Spivey reaching up to her. It wouldn't go away.

Olivia felt around for her shoes. They must have fallen off when he pushed her down the stairs. She felt cold and damp. She grabbed the blanket and wrapped it around herself. Tears streamed down her face. Why had she come on this miserable trip? She should've just stayed home.

Chapter 10

RACHEL PULLED HER cellphone out of her purse. "Hold on, Mother. You're talking way too fast for this time of day. I just woke up. What are you saying?"

Her mother explained that Olivia was expected to be home the previous day, and here it was nine in the morning, and she still wasn't back.

"Mother, you sound like you're having some kind of panic attack. I'm sure she's just having a good time. They probably decided to stay another night. Think about it. She's finally out of the house, and she's with her new boyfriend." Rachel smiled. She should be so lucky.

Her mother said that it wasn't like her sister not to keep in touch, and that if something had changed, Olivia would have called her with their new plans.

"I'm sure she tried to call you. Do you know where she went? It's way up north. It's in the mountains. They probably don't have any cellphone towers up there. Look, why don't you try and get some rest. If you don't hear from her by this afternoon, let me know. I'll stop by and we can talk about it then. Okay?"

Rachel put her phone away and opened the refrigerator. She curled her nose. Oh, those leftovers had to go. Disappointed that there was nothing to eat, she slammed the door shut. Maybe she should call Bobby. He was always good about taking her out to breakfast.

Arnold entered the room that girl and her boyfriend had been staying in and glanced around. The room was tidy. She must have packed up everything in that suitcase of hers that was still sitting in the foyer. With her boyfriend taking off on her like he did, how was she planning on getting home? Wait a minute. That's why she came down the stairs. To ask them how she could find a way home. Maybe she was going to ask him to drive her to the bus depot. That wouldn't have worked. It was forty miles away.

He walked out, locked the door behind him, and returned to the foyer. Arnold opened her suitcase and sifted through the contents. He held up a sheer, black negligee. Oh, yeah. She'd look great in that. He tossed it back into the suitcase and closed the lid.

Kay Bloomfield's eyes were wide. "Someone broke into your house? Thursday night and you're just telling me now?"

"I was busy," Leslie said. "That's why I asked you to have lunch with me today instead of Tuesday."

"What did the cops say? Did they catch the guy?"

Leslie poured cream into her coffee. "Catch him? Hardly. I swear, the cop they sent over looked just like bumbling Barney Fife. I mean, it was everything I could do just to keep from laughing. His uniform was two sizes too big, and he didn't seem to have a clue as to what to do."

"Did they dust for fingerprints?"

Leslie rolled her eyes. "Are you kidding? All he did was ask me a few questions. When I told him nothing was taken,

73

and I didn't get a good look at the guy, he seemed to lose interest. He just flipped his notebook shut and left."

Kay picked up a french fry. "I bet I know who it was."

"Who?"

"Your friend, Creepy Creeperton."

Leslie looked at her. "Who?"

"You know. The guy that follows us around every Tuesday."

"Arnold? You think Arnold broke into my house?" Leslie laughed. "He's afraid of his own shadow. I don't think he'd have the guts to be breaking into anybody's place. Besides, his mother would kill him."

"I don't know." Kay looked around. "He'll probably show up any minute."

"You're crazy."

Olivia lay on the mattress and stared into the darkness. The deadbolt clicked. There was a scraping sound. She covered her eyes as bright light engulfed the room.

Arnold stepped in and threw her suitcase on the floor. "Here's your things."

She stood up. "Can I go now?"

He took a step toward her. "No."

"Please! I have to go. My mother's very sick, and she's expecting me back. I'm supposed to be taking care of her. This whole stupid trip was a horrible mistake." She looked up at him. "Why...why are you doing this?"

"Because you saw something you shouldn't have, and I need to figure out what to do with you."

Olivia glanced over at chains that were fastened to the wall and then to another wall that was covered with pictures. "It looks like this room was...ready for something."

Arnold's eyes narrowed. "It's a long story. It doesn't have anything to do with you."

She started shaking. "Please let me go. I...I won't say anything."

"What happened was an accident. A terrible accident. Mother grabbed me where I'd hurt my arm. I jumped back and hit the stove. A pan fell off and burned her. I...I just freaked out. She's always hated me. Ridiculed me. She..." He rubbed his forehead. "Oh, who the hell cares? I...I...gotta think about this." He pushed the small door open and disappeared.

As the door was closing, Olivia screamed, "The lights. Can you leave the lights on? Please!"

She held her breath and waited for them to go off. They didn't. She didn't move for half an hour. Her heart was beating fast. She examined her confinement area more closely. Insulated walls. It looked like there had been an opening at the far end once, but now it was boarded up with thick sheets of plywood. That's where the sliver of light had been. She walked over and pushed on the boards. They didn't budge. Pieces of insulation had been fastened to the walls. No sound was going to escape from this nasty room.

She walked over to the pictures. A few of the pictures were old. They looked like yearbook photos. The rest all looked as if they had been taken around the same time. Different outfits, but her age looked like it hadn't changed. Were they all of the same girl?

Who was she? Had she been put in this room too? Olivia searched for any signs that another person had been imprisoned there. Were there any words written on the wall? Pieces of clothing? She didn't find anything.

Olivia returned to the mattress, pulled the thin blanket up to her, and trembled uncontrollably.

Duck pulled over onto the shoulder of M-64 and peered into the woods. Could this possibly be the road? He had been told to turn right eight and a half miles west of the Welcome to Ontonagon sign. The man had mentioned that the road was narrow and would be hard to find, but this looked more like some cow path. The term road was quite an overstatement.

Duck wasn't thinking right. The back of his head was still sore where he had landed on the floor. Did he look too foolish with that big bandage still wrapped around his head? The doctor had been reluctant to discharge him from the hospital that morning. Should he have stayed home? A bad concussion and some blood loss weren't anything to fool with, and he still felt weak.

He fingered the bandage. Wait until they got a look at him. He'd be lucky if they didn't slam the door in his face. He hoped not. Based on how the people from Marquette had gone on and on, this might be the opportunity of a lifetime.

He made a quick turn and held on tight to the steering wheel as the car bounced along the path. After half a mile the large wrought-iron gate he'd been told to look for came into view. He pulled up to a small black box and pressed a button.

A deep voice resonated from the speaker. "Yes?"

"Duck...I mean Dennis Lindquist, the jewelry guy's here." There was a beeping noise and both sides of the heavy gate slowly swung open.

He drove another few hundred feet and pulled up in front of a huge, three-story stone edifice that looked like it should have been standing in the middle of a winery in the French countryside.

He stepped out of the car and admired the structure.

A large wooden door swung open and a man approached. "Thank you for coming. My name is Dieter." His eyes narrowed.

Duck smiled as the man looked him over. Duck wanted to say, "You should have seen the other guy," but he restrained himself.

Dieter asked, "Are you… all right?"

"Yes, yes. Just a slight accident. A little concussion, but I'm fine." Probably wouldn't be a good idea to tell him he'd been in a bar fight.

Dieter cocked his head and stared at Dennis again. Finally he said, "Come. I'll show you where you will work."

Duck sighed. Thank goodness. He had the job. He stepped inside. What accent did Dieter have? German?

He followed Dieter from the cavernous foyer into a dark-paneled dining room. As they walked beside a long, highly polished table, Duck counted the chairs. Twenty-four. Twelve on each side.

Dieter turned to the right and pointed to another room. "The sitting room is here, next to the library. I've set up a desk for you to work at. The water closet is at the end of the library, should you need to use the facilities."

Duck glanced around. A thick canvas cloth was spread over the desk. An even larger one covered the floor beneath. The desk was set in a small alcove with floor-to-ceiling windows behind it. A blue drapery was tied open on each side of the window. The room had a stone fireplace on the left. Mounted above it was a huge oil painting of a stormy sea crashing against a tall cliff. Three groupings of overstuffed chairs sat around mahogany tables. A long sofa covered in silk fabric stood against the far wall.

Dieter pointed to a wall next to the desk. "There are electrical outlets on that wall, should you need them." He picked up a small metal chest and raised the top. "You can start with this batch. Some repairs are needed, and Mrs. Haverhill would like everything to be thoroughly cleaned."

Duck gasped. Just from a quick glance, he could tell the jewelry was very old and very expensive. Maybe *expensive* wasn't the correct term. *Priceless* was more like it. He gave a slight cough and turned to Dieter. "Yes, well then, let me go to the car and get my tools."

Arms full, on his way back he noticed a young woman ahead of him in the hallway. She was wearing a tight servant's uniform. Her long, dark hair bobbed from side to side as she retreated from his view.

"That was Juliette."

Duck jumped. He hadn't noticed Dieter behind him.

"She will be serving you lunch at noon."

"Oh, thank you. That will be nice." Duck made his way back to the sitting room and set his tools carefully on the desk. He removed all of the jewelry from the box and made two piles. One group needed to be repaired and the others that only needed cleaning.

After two hours footsteps sounded near the doorway. Duck looked up as Juliette stepped into the sitting room. She was balancing a large silver tray of sandwiches and a carafe of coffee.

"*Monsieur*, l have prepared *la dejeuner* for you."

"Excuse me?"

She smiled. "Oh, pardon, *Monsieur*. Lunch. I have prepared lunch for you. Follow me to the library."

Duck watched her tight uniform sway as she walked. When they entered the library, Juliette set the tray down on a table and stared at his bandage.

He smiled. "Slight accident. But I'm fine now."

She made a small bow and left the room.

As he ate alone, Duck marveled at the plushness of his surroundings and the beautiful woman who had served him.

Arnold's mother wouldn't budge. After futilely tugging and pulling at her several times with his good arm, Arnold sat on a kitchen chair and struggled to catch his breath. He was drenched in sweat. His injured arm seemed to be getting worse. He had managed to drag his mother closer to her bedroom door, but now she was wedged between the hall and the doorway. With only one of his arms working, it was impossible to move her any farther or return her to where she had been.

He went into the living room and lowered the shades. Earlier that morning he had called everyone who had a reservation for the next few weeks and told them there had been a fire, and they would have to find other accommodations. He had also taped a CLOSED sign to the front door.

Arnold returned and attempted to move his mother again. It was impossible. He needed help. She couldn't remain in the hall forever.

He went down to his room in the basement, picked up a hunting knife, stuck it inside his belt, and headed over to the coal bin. He unlocked the door, pushed up the thick two-by-four brace, and stepped inside.

Olivia was sitting on the mattress. She scooted away from him.

"You're going to have to help me, and don't even think of doing anything stupid." He pointed to his belt. "I have a knife." He grabbed her by the arm and pulled her to her feet.

"Help you with what?"

"Move my mother."

She pulled away. "No!"

He grabbed her again. This time much harder. "This is not a request." He pushed her out the door and almost had to drag her up the stairs.

As they neared his mother's body, Olivia looked away.

Arnold reached down and grabbed his mother's arm. "Go ahead. Take her legs."

Olivia shut her eyes and took a step backward. "Please. I can't do this."

"Do it! Don't make me have to use this knife on you."

She bent down and took hold of Mrs. Spivey's ankles. She shuddered. They were cold.

He grunted, "We're going to drag her down the back steps and out to the barn." He pulled the corpse toward the kitchen.

When they got to the back door, he stopped. His arm was aching. He leaned against the door and tried to ignore the pain.

"Okay, let's go." He pushed the door open, and they dragged the body out onto the back porch. Arnold went down several steps and tugged on his mother's arm. The body slowly began to slide down the wooden steps.

Olivia let go and fell backward onto the porch.

Mrs. Spivey slowly slid down the steps, gaining speed along the way. Arnold tried to slow down the movement, but the body slammed into him and knocked him off the stairs.

Olivia leaped up, jumped over the railing, and ran toward the woods. "Help! Help me!"

Arnold stumbled over his mother's corpse and chased after her.

As she sprinted for a clump of white birch trees, he caught up to her, grabbed her by the hair, and slammed her to the ground. He reached into his belt and pulled out his knife. "I...I don't want to hurt you, but if you try that again, I'll cut your throat. I will, dammit! You can scream as loud as you want out here. It won't do you any good. My closest neighbor's a mile and a half away. He's seventy-eight years old and deaf as a stone. Nobody's going to hear you."

He yanked her to her feet and led her back to his mother's body where they continued to drag her over to the barn. Arnold pointed to some tall grass. "Over here."

Rachel sat at her mother's bedside and held her hand. She had been shocked to see that her mother's condition had taken a turn for the worse. Rachel looked at the clock. It was almost 8 p.m. "You shouldn't be so worried, Mother. A friend of mine spent some time up around that area, and he said the phone service sucked. He couldn't get a signal anywhere. But he told me it was awesome up there with the mountains and all the trees. They probably decided to spend another day or two, and she didn't have any way to let you know."

Her mother squeezed her hand. "I hope you're right."

"I'm sure that's what's happening. I'm going to talk with Elaine. I smell fresh coffee. You want a cup?"

Her mother shook her head and closed her eyes.

Rachel left the room and took a chair across from her mother's neighbor. "She's trying to sleep."

81

"Good. This worry has taken a toll on her." Elaine fidgeted with a napkin. "I wish Olivia would call us. God knows what could have happened. They could have driven off the side of a mountain or something."

Rachel dug in her purse for a cigarette. "Oh, no. Not you too. How about, Olivia's having the time of her life, and she wanted to stay another day. My friend told me the cellphone service up there is bad. I'm sure she tried to call."

Elaine's eyes widened. "You can't smoke in here. Please. Go outside."

Rachel stood up and grabbed her purse. "How 'bout I just head home."

"Home? Did you see how feeble your mother is?"

"She's sleeping now. It's Saturday night. I got plans. I'll stop over for lunch tomorrow. Olivia will probably be home by then, or at least let us know she's on her way."

Elaine watched in amazement as Rachel stuck the cigarette in her mouth and headed out the door.

Paul set a beer down in front of Charlie and said, "Duck just walked in. We need to hear about his new job."

Charlie turned. "Oh, yeah. I forgot about that."

Duck spotted them and took a seat. He looked around. "Pretty slow for a Saturday night. I stopped over at Sudsy's. They got a bigger crowd."

"That's because they've got a band tonight," Paul said.

"You're right. Why don't you have one here?" Duck asked.

Paul shrugged. "Why bother? We're history in about ten weeks."

"A damn car wash. Can you believe it?" Charlie tossed ten dollars on the bar. "Buy our friend here a beer so we can hear all about his visit to the Haverhill mansion."

Duck's eyes lit up. "Oh, yeah. You guys are going to love this."

Paul poured a draft beer and set it down in front of Duck. "Before you start, how's your head?"

Duck reached back and gently touched the bandage. "It's better. I'm taking this damn thing off tomorrow."

"Good," Paul replied. "It's bad for business. Now, about that mansion. What's it like? Is it all decaying and falling apart?"

"Hardly. It's a French chateau complete with chandeliers, thick drapes hanging from the windows, all kinds of fancy couches, and chairs covered in silk. You name it, it's there. A guy told me they took it apart in France, shipped it over here, and put it back together again, stone by stone."

"Wow," Charlie said. "Sounds like a lot of work to me. Why wouldn't they just—"

Duck interrupted, "Oh! I almost forgot the most important part." He paused, grabbed his beer, and took a long drink.

"What?" Charlie asked.

"It comes with its own French maid. And what a maid she is." He rubbed his hands together. "Ooh la la!"

"No kidding," Paul said. "I've never seen a French maid come walking in here."

Duck laughed. "And you probably won't. This babe's real classy. And cute too. She brought me a great lunch. I must have looked like a fool because I couldn't stop staring at her. Dieter, a big German guy who works there, gave me the hairy eyeball, so I had to stop gawking. He looked at me like I had just violated his wife or something."

"Are you going back?" Charlie asked.

Duck nodded. "Oh, yeah. They got a lot of work for me. I fixed a bunch of stuff. Man, you should see what I was working on. It looked like the crown jewels from some Balkan country. And there's a bunch more, so they tell me. I can't wait to go back."

Paul got Charlie another beer. "You just want to see that French girl again."

"No shit! You'd want to go back too, if you ever saw her.

Charlie asked, "What about old Mrs. Haverhill. Did you see her?"

"Nope. Nowhere to be seen. But it wasn't like I was roaming around the place or anything. They had a table set up for me in the sitting room, and that's where I stayed. Well, that and the library."

"They got a library?" Paul asked.

Duck's eyebrows shot up. "They sure do. Every wall covered with books. Big leather chairs scattered around. That's where the French maid serves me lunch." He laughed. "Can you believe it? A French maid serving me lunch. I tell you, it's like nothing I ever thought would be around here."

Chapter 11

THUNDER RUMBLED IN the distance. Rachel's raincoat hung over the back of a kitchen chair, dripping water onto the floor.

"You have to go to the police," Joyce said to her daughter.

Rachel frowned. "The police? She's probably just having a few more days with her new boyfriend."

"I don't know about that. Something has to be done," Elaine said. "We're tired of sitting around here wondering where she is. Here it is, Sunday morning. She was supposed to be back home Friday."

Rachel drummed her long fingernails on the kitchen table. "How about this. I know some of her friends, but I don't have their phone numbers with me. I'm going to go home, call them, and see what they know about this trip. Maybe one of them has heard from her." She looked at the two concerned women. "How's that?"

Her mother turned to Elaine. "I guess it's okay. At least it's a starting place."

Elaine glanced at the clock. "But we'll need to hear from you by three. If we don't, I'll be going down to the police department myself."

"I'll be back in a few hours," Rachel promised. "Then we can all decide what to do next. I'm hoping Olivia will march in here right after I leave so we can forget about this whole mess." She stood up. "Oh, what's her boyfriend's name? Maybe one of the girls has his phone number. Then I can call him too."

Joyce looked at Elaine. "I...I can't remember. I know she introduced him to me." She thought for a moment. "Bobby? Was that it? No, Tommy! Yes, she called him Tommy."

"Tommy what?" Rachel asked.

Her mother looked down at the table. "I don't know. They were in such a hurry. He was in and out in a matter of seconds. I can't remember if I even got his last name." She looked up at Rachel with tears in her eyes. "I'm sorry."

"That's okay, Mom. I'm sure one of the girls will know."

Driving home, Rachel tried to remember Olivia's closest girlfriends. There was Caitlin Burnett, Sandy Moberg, Samantha McGuire, and Lindsey...what was her last name? Hopefully one of them would be able to provide some information about Olivia's trip and her boyfriend.

She climbed the rickety steps to her apartment and paged through her address book. She could only find numbers for Caitlin and Samantha. She scribbled them down on a piece of paper and decided to have lunch downstairs at the bar.

Sitting at a table with a vodka tonic, Rachel wondered what to say. She didn't want to sound panicky or have the girls think that she was sneaking around behind Olivia's back checking on her. She decided to stop overthinking it. She punched in Caitlin's number.

"Hi, Caitlin. It's me, Rachel Lewis, Olivia's sister. I'm fine. Hey, I was wondering if you knew anything about her trip to the Porcupine Mountains." She waited for a response. "No?

Yeah, I was kind of surprised when I heard she was going there myself. She went with a guy named Tommy. Do you know him?"

Rachel pursed her lips. "You don't like him? None of her friends like him either?" She took a big sip of her drink. "You don't happen to know his last name, do you?" She grabbed a pencil from her purse. "Riggins? Is that spelled R-i-g-g-i-n-s?"

She scribbled his name on a napkin. "Do you know where he lives? Oh, someplace downstate. Do you know where? No, that's okay. How about his phone number? No, nothing's wrong. Thank you so much for talking with me."

She set the phone down on the table. The conversation wasn't very encouraging. All of Olivia's friends hated Tommy? That sounded a little dramatic. Maybe Caitlin had gone out with him first, and she was mad at him or something.

Rachel picked up the phone again and dialed Samantha's number. When she didn't answer, Rachel left her name and number and tossed the phone into her purse.

The bartender walked over with a big hamburger and an order of french fries. "Here you are, Rach. You want another drink?"

"Sure." She looked around at the nearly empty bar. "Sit down, Bobby. I'd like to talk to you for a minute."

"Okay." He pulled out a chair and joined her. "What's on your mind?"

"Have you ever been up north to the Porcupine Mountains?"

He shook his head. "No, always thought it would be a good trip, but I never made it. Why?"

She handed him a french fry. "My sister went up there with some guy. They were supposed to come back two days ago. I'm...I'm starting to get worried."

He grabbed another fry. "Two days ago? Yeah, I'd be worried too. It's supposed to be pretty wild up there. Nothing but woods for miles. It's a wilderness area. Maybe they had a wreck. Have you called any hospitals?"

She closed her eyes. "No, but I guess that's what I'll do next."

Bobby stood up. "Good luck. Yeah, I think you'd better start calling hospitals."

As he went back to the bar, her cellphone rang. It was Samantha calling her back. After talking for a few minutes, it was clear that Samantha liked Tommy even less than Caitlin did. But she did have his home phone number.

Rachel punched in the number and listened as it rang over and over. After nine rings she hung up. She slowly picked at her lunch. She didn't have much of an appetite. If she were going to start calling hospitals, she wanted to do that in the privacy of her apartment. She left money for the bill on the table and returned upstairs.

Two hours later, Rachel finally finished her calls. No hospital or police agency within fifty miles of the Porcupine Mountains had a record of interacting with her sister. That was a huge relief, but what Olivia's friends had told her about her boyfriend was troubling. She would definitely not be sharing that with her mother.

Rachel looked at the clock. It was about the time they were expecting her to return. She hurried down the stairs. Maybe by the time she got to Mother's, Olivia would be there.

It was quiet when she entered the house. Too quiet. Her mother was sleeping. Elaine was sitting at the kitchen table doing a crossword puzzle. Rachel looked around. "She's not here?"

Elaine frowned. "No, did you find out anything?"

Rachel lowered her voice. "I did. But you can't tell Mother."

A look of alarm crossed Elaine's face. "Oh, God. What is it?"

"It's not that bad, but from what I've been told, my sister's friends weren't very happy with her new boyfriend."

"They weren't?"

"No, and now I'm worried. But, on a good note, I called as many hospitals and police departments as I could find, and nobody's heard anything bad about them."

"I guess that's good news," Elaine said.

"It is. But I wish we knew more about that boyfriend of hers."

Joyce appeared in the doorway. "What about her boyfriend?"

Both women turned.

Rachel answered, "I was telling Elaine that I wish we knew more about her boyfriend. I learned that he lives somewhere downstate, but I don't know where."

Her mother took a seat at the kitchen table. "Oh. I asked him when he picked her up. He said he was from Lansing."

"Really." Rachel glanced at the clock. "I think I'm going to drive up to the mountains and see if I can find out where she's staying."

Her mother looked surprised. "You are? When?"

"Now. But, I'm going to need some money."

"Now? You mean right now?" her mother asked incredulously.

Rachel stood up. "Yes."

"What happened? What have you found out? This morning you thought we were both overreacting. Now you're about to drive up there looking for her. Something changed your mind. What was it?"

"Nothing, Mother. But the more I think about it, the more I don't think this is like Olivia. You're right. She's very conscientious. There's no way she'd be two days late and not find some way to let us know what's going on."

"Okay," her mother said. "Let me get you some money."

As she disappeared into the bedroom, Elaine said, "I'm so glad you're going up there. Your mother and I are worried sick." She paused. "But…where are you going to look?"

Rachel shrugged. "I have no idea."

Her mother returned and handed her some bills. "Here's a hundred dollars. I'm sorry, but that's all I can spare."

"Thank you."

"I brought you a book," Arnold said, handing it to Olivia.

She stared at the floor and didn't respond.

He set it down at the end of the mattress. "It's science fiction. I don't know if you like that kind of stuff, but I do. It's a cool book."

She continued to look down at the floor.

Arnold picked up her suitcase and opened it. "I'm trying to be nice to you, but if that's the way you want to be, I can change my tune." He pulled out the black lace teddy and threw it at her. "Put this on."

She looked up at him. "What? I'm not putting that on."

His neck got warm. "You…you…better do what I say." He grabbed her by the arm and dragged her over to the wall. He wrapped a chain around her wrist, snapped a lock shut, and pulled on the chain to make sure it stayed secure. "Are you happy now?"

He returned to the suitcase, picked up the lace teddy, and shoved it into his pocket. "The next time I come down here, you'd better put this on when I tell you to."

He went over to the door and stopped. "You know something? I'm very disappointed in your boyfriend selection."

Olivia turned her head toward the cool, damp, concrete blocks.

"I did a little research on him on the Internet. Quite the guy. Dishonorable discharge for molesting a female recruit, domestic battery on his ex-wife, at least three assault charges. You sure know how to pick 'em." He pushed the door open. "You should be glad I saved you from that creep."

The door slammed shut, and the lights, which had been on since the day before, turned off. Olivia sat chained to the wall in total darkness.

It was almost nine o'clock at night when Rachel stepped into her room at the White Pine Motel in Ontonagon. The drive had been uneventful except for three deer she had seen on the way. The motel wasn't very fancy, but it was inexpensive. She tossed her small suitcase on the bed and stared out the window overlooking the parking lot. Where should she start? She had called Tommy's number several times on the way, but there had never been an answer.

She pulled out a picture of Olivia and stared at it for a moment. It had been taken the year before on Olivia's eighteenth birthday. Tears blurred her vision. They hadn't always gotten along, but she was her sister. Rachel stuck it back into her purse and headed to the door.

There was a bar next to the motel, which was one of the reasons, besides the price, she had decided to stay there.

She walked over to the building and glanced at the sign. Sudsy's. She went in and took a seat at the bar. When a man came over to take her order, Rachel pulled out the photograph and handed it to him. "Can I ask you a question? Have you seen this girl?"

The bartender stared at it. "I don't think so. She doesn't look familiar." He handed it back. "What's the story? She steal your boyfriend or something?"

"No, she's my sister. She came up here about a week ago, and she should have been home by now. I'm trying to find out where she is."

"Let me take another look." He picked up the picture again. "No, I think I'd remember her." He handed it back. "I'm only part-time. You may want to show it to Ray when he comes in. He works the shifts I'm off."

Rachel stuck the picture back into her purse. "Is there a restaurant open around here?"

"No. Everything in town closes up around eight o'clock at the latest. But I can get you a burger." He handed her a menu. "It's mostly bar food, but we serve until eleven."

She looked over the menu. "Okay. I'll have the Burger Deluxe and a beer."

Since it was a Sunday night, the place wasn't very busy which gave Rachel time to talk to the bartender a little more. When she asked him if he could suggest a few places where her sister might be staying, he rattled off a list. The Scotts Motel, the Northern Motel, Superior Bed and Breakfast, Mountain Vista, and the Coppertop Camping and RV Resort. She held up her hand. "Hold it. There's no way my sister would ever stay at a campground."

Rachel scribbled down the motel names on a napkin, finished her hamburger, and had two more beers. The long day, combined with the tension of not knowing what she might find, kicked in. She was exhausted. She paid her tab, walked back to the motel, and went to bed.

The next morning on her way out of the motel, she stopped at the reception desk and showed Olivia's picture to the man who was working behind the counter. He didn't recognize the girl in the photograph, but he did recommend a place for breakfast.

Rachel spent the morning visiting the places the bartender had mentioned. The town was so small, most of the motels were located within a seven mile radius. People at the first three places claimed they had never seen her. Nobody had been able to give her any information.

According to the desk clerk at the Superior Bed and Breakfast, the last place on her list was only two miles away.

As she headed down the road, she drove by a sign for the Porcupine Mountains State Wilderness Visitor Center. Maybe somebody there had seen her. If she were going to go hiking, it would make sense that Olivia and her boyfriend would stop at the visitor's center.

Rachel made a U-turn and pulled into the parking lot. There were several people walking around the exhibits when she stepped into the main room.

She pulled out her picture and walked up to one of the couples. "Excuse me, have you seen this woman?"

They both peered down at the photograph. "No," the man said. "But we just got here. Did she get lost on one of the trails?"

"I don't know. She's been missing for a few days."

He gave her a nervous smile and stepped away. She was about to approach another couple when a woman behind the counter asked, "Did you say someone was lost?"

"No, I'm looking for my sister. I'm not sure what happened to her. I know she came up here to go hiking, but that's about all I know."

"Have you reported this to the staff up at headquarters?"

"No, I never even thought of this place until I passed a sign down the road." She handed her Olivia's picture.

"I've seen her," the woman responded.

Rachel's heart leapt. "What! You have? When?"

"She came in a few days ago with a very rude young man. He was all upset because they saw Prospector Pete. He wanted us to arrest him."

"Who's Prospector Pete?"

"An old man who lives in the woods. Nobody knows what his real name is, so everyone around here calls him Prospector Pete. He's harmless, but your sister's boyfriend got real nasty." The woman turned to the door. "Hello. Welcome to the Visitor Center. If you have any questions, just ask."

She turned back to Rachel. "It's none of my business, but between you and me, I think your sister needs to find a new man."

Rachel shuddered. That was now three out of three. Every woman who met Olivia's boyfriend seemed to hate him on sight. "Did they happen to mention where they were staying?"

The woman shook her head. "No, they just wanted us to go after old Pete."

Still holding on to Olivia's picture, Rachel returned to her car. One more stop. The last place on the bartender's list.

The parking lot for the Mountain Vista Motel was all gravel. When Rachel stepped out of the car and looked around, she understood how the place got its name. The view was spectacular.

She approached the desk and held out her photograph. "Excuse me, sir, but have you seen this woman?"

The clerk, a man in his mid-to-late thirties, glanced down at the picture. "Hmm. No, can't say that I have, but I wish I would have. She's quite the looker." He returned his gaze to Rachel. "And look at you." He smiled. "You need a room? I'll give you a great deal."

"No thank you. I'm staying someplace else. I'm looking for this girl." She held the picture closer to the man's face. "Are you sure you haven't seen her?"

"Like I said, lady, when I see a beautiful woman like her, or yourself I might add, I remember them. Can I get you a cup of coffee?" He stepped out from behind the desk, put his arm around her, and pointed to a faded couch. "Maybe you'd like to sit for a minute and tell me all about the girl you're looking for."

He had moved in a little too close for Rachel's comfort. "Ah, I don't think so. I really have to be on my way."

The man took hold of her arm. "How about a drink tonight? I could meet you in town. We could go have dinner. How does that sound?"

She pulled away. "No thanks."

She pushed the lobby door open and hurried to her car. Once inside, she locked the doors. What was that about? Talk about a creep. That guy was coming on to her faster than a car without brakes barreling down the mountain.

Rachel was still fuming when she pulled into town. She stopped at an IGA store and picked up some bread, a package of cold cuts, a bottle of mustard, and a twelve pack of beer.

Back at the motel she made two sandwiches and popped open a beer. She flipped on the television and found an old movie. Three beers later, she was sprawled on top of the bed sleeping soundly.

Olivia sat on the mattress and took a bite from the hamburger Arnold had given her. She wondered how close the McDonald's was. Almost everything he had brought her to eat had been in a McDonald's bag.

She rubbed her wrist. It was red and tender from where the metal shackle had been attached.

He also brought a plastic lawn chair with him, in which he was now sitting.

She took a drink of her soda. Was that a towel he had made into a sling for his arm?

He asked, "Have you ever heard of the Stockholm Syndrome?"

She shook her head.

"Well, it's really quite interesting. Some people were taken hostage during a bank robbery in Sweden, and, over time, they came to like their captors."

Olivia almost choked on a piece of meat.

"I know it sounds strange, but once they were freed, they wouldn't even testify against them." He stared at her. "I'm hoping that's what happens here. I'll bring you books and good things to eat. I'll be nice to you, and you should be nice to me."

He pulled the black teddy out of his back pocket. "Like putting this on."

She pushed the McDonalds bag away. "Let me go, and I won't say anything. My mother's sick. I have to get back home and take care of her."

He stood up. "I've waited long enough." He grabbed her wrist and yanked her to her feet. A half-filled container of vanilla milkshake fell over and spilled on the mattress.

She tried to pull away from him as he drew her closer. Holding her tight with his right hand, he fumbled at the buttons of her blouse with the hand that was in the sling.

She pulled away again. His arm. Go for his injured arm. She made a fist and smashed it into Arnold's sling.

He screamed, fell back, and cradled his arm. It took him a few seconds before he could speak. "Damn you! Just wait. You're another bitch just like my mother, and you saw what happened to her. Your time is coming. And…and you can forget me spending any more money on food for you."

He stumbled out of the small enclosure and slammed the door shut. The lights flickered and the room was plunged into darkness.

Charlie Loonsfoot sat at a conference table with five other park managers. A lieutenant from the State Police Crime Lab was connecting his computer to a projector. He signaled for the lights to be lowered and then flashed a picture on the screen.

"Gentlemen, I know you've been patiently waiting for an update on the Summit Peak Trail findings. It has been determined that the skull and remains are of the same individual. After the skull was found, our team, along with several of your park rangers, extensively searched the area upstream from where the skull was discovered. After several days one of our cadaver dogs found the burial site. The body was only under a foot of dirt. We believe the victim, a woman between the ages of approximately seventeen to twenty-six, was probably killed elsewhere and buried up on the mountain sometime in the spring.

"We have a forensic anthropologist doing a full facial reconstruction of the skull. Once his work is finished, we'll distribute the results to the news media, and we'll post flyers over a fifty mile radius to see if anyone recognizes her. Do you have any questions?"

Charlie raised his hand. "Could this be the work of a serial killer?"

The lieutenant glanced down at his notes. "We don't think so. We haven't had any reports of anyone else who's missing, so for right now we think this may be a one-off murder. Possibly a crime of passion. We don't know."

Charlie's boss stood up. "Well, we thank you for the update, Lieutenant. As always, we're ready to cooperate with your department any way we can."

Duck sat at his work desk and peered at an emerald through a jeweler's loop. He pushed the loop up on his forehead and rubbed his eyes. The amount of rare and expensive jewelry he had seen was almost impossible to comprehend and he knew there was more. From what Dieter said, he'd be working here for at least another week.

Juliette poked her head into the doorway. "*Monsieur* Duck, are you ready for lunch?"

He smiled. "Is it that time already?" His eyes followed her as she walked in carrying a silver tray. He stood up, stretched, and followed her to the library.

Juliette put the tray down on one of the tables and was about to leave when Duck motioned for her to join him.

She glanced behind her. "Dieter, he will not be happy if he sees me sitting with you."

Duck waved his hand. "Forget about him. I want to hear more about what you were telling me yesterday.

"About Toulouse?"

"Yes, it sounds like such a fascinating city."

She smiled and took his hand as she sat down. "You remembered?"

"Of course I remembered. You said it's near the border with Spain, and that it's called the Rose City because of all the pink bricks they build things with."

"Oh, *mon dieu*! You are such a good listener."

Duck took a big bite of his sandwich. He could listen to her all day.

A dark shadow crossed the table as Dieter entered the room. "Your chores, they must be all completed, ya?"

Juliette jumped up. "I was just making sure our guest approved of his lunch."

"Guest?" Dieter asked. "I'm sure the tradesman has everything he needs."

As Juliette hurriedly left the room, Dieter turned, gave him a warning look, and followed her out the door.

Duck threw down his sandwich. What a jerk.

Chapter 12

A KNOCK ON the door woke Rachel from a deep sleep. She threw on a bathrobe, went to the door, and peered out the small security peephole. It was the desk clerk from downstairs. He looked agitated and wet. Behind him rain poured down at an angle.

She slid the door chain into place and cracked open the door. "Can I help you?"

"Sorry to bother you, ma'am, but you're the girl looking for her sister, right?"

Rachel's heart beat faster. "Yes, do you have some—"

He interrupted. "I think you better turn on the TV right away. They've found something that you should know about."

She froze. Found something? She ran to the television and flipped it on.

The desk clerk yelled through the crack in the door. "Channel Two."

She grabbed the remote. A commercial for a scenic boat ride to Isle Royal National Park was just ending. A man sitting behind a news desk filled the screen. "We have breaking news that human remains have been found up in The Porcupine Mountain State Wilderness Area. There is speculation that the skull found near the Summit Peak Trail has been associated with the remains, but we are awaiting confirmation from forensic experts to confirm those rumors. We will keep you posted on any new developments."

Lightheaded, she eased herself onto the edge of the bed. Human remains? A skull?

"Are you okay, miss?"

Trying not to cry, she stepped over to the door, unlatched the chain, and let the desk clerk in.

"I'm sorry to be the bearer of such bad news, but I thought since you were searching for someone, you should know what they found up on the mountain." He disappeared into the bathroom and returned with a glass of water. "Here."

"Thank you." She took a sip.

"My name's Walter. We met when you checked in."

Rachel handed the glass back to him. Her hands were trembling. "Yes, I remember. Why didn't anyone tell me they found…found something up on the mountain?"

Walter sat down at the desk. "I never thought of it. It was a while back. They found the skull last month. Sounds like they just found the rest of the body a few days ago. Time goes by. We get busy. It never occurred to me to say anything."

She jumped up. "Wait a minute. You said the skull was found in June?"

Walter nodded. "Something like that."

Rachel picked up a magazine and fanned herself. "Thank goodness! Olivia left to come up here last Tuesday. If they found someone's skull a month ago, it couldn't possibly be her."

Walter turned toward the door. "I'm sorry I gave you such a fright. Looks like I came barging up here with terrible news for nothing. I'm sorry. Please forgive me."

Rachel tried to stop shaking. "It wasn't your fault. You did the right thing. You're about the only person I've met around here who seems to care about what happened to my sister. Thank you."

He reached for the door. "I better be getting back down to the front desk."

After he left, Rachel took a long, hot shower. She got dressed and used the tiny coffee pot to make some coffee. She glanced out the window at the parking lot. What a nasty morning. By the looks of those puddles, it must have rained all night. She closed the curtain and flipped through the thin telephone book she had found in the night stand next to the bed. Not counting the campgrounds, there were only two other motels listed that the bartender at Sudsy's hadn't told her about. They were both east of the small town where she was staying, which was in the opposite direction and far from the State Wilderness area.

She looked out the window. The wind had died down, and the rain had turned to a light mist. Only two more places to check. Might as well get it over with. Rachel grabbed her jacket and ran to the car. She jumped into the car and pulled her keys from her purse. Was she wasting her time? Should she go to the police and file a missing person's report? Her mother had almost done the same thing the weekend Rachel ran off to a concert in Milwaukee with her boyfriend. After the concert they had decided to stay and see some friends. She had never thought to call her mother and tell her the new plans. Remember how mad Mom was when she finally walked into the house that next Tuesday. Rachel smiled. No, no police report yet.

By the time Rachel arrived at the first motel, the rain had picked up again. She sprinted to the lobby.

A woman in her mid-thirties sat smoking a cigarette. She looked up from a soap opera magazine. "Can I help you? We got plenty of rooms." She turned to the window. "This rain's put a stop to just about everything."

Rachel pulled out Olivia's picture. "I'm not looking for a room. I'm looking for my sister." She held out the photograph.

The clerk stared at it for a long time and then shook her head. "She doesn't look familiar, but people come and go all the time. When would she have stayed here?"

"She would have arrived Tuesday, July 8th, and stayed for a few days."

The woman shrugged. "Like I said, we see a lot of people." She handed the photograph back. "Sorry, she doesn't look familiar."

Rachel sighed. "Okay. Thank you for your time."

The last motel was four miles down a narrow, two-lane blacktop road. Rounding a sharp curve, Rachel slammed on the brakes. A bear cub was sauntering across the road. It turned to look at her and then disappeared into a thick crop of bushes. Bears? Oh no! Could that be possible? Did Olivia and Tommy stumble upon a bear on one of the hiking trails? No, she couldn't think about something like that.

By the time Rachel found the last motel, it had stopped raining. One tiny patch of blue sky was visible through the gray clouds.

She pulled up to the lobby and turned off the engine. The place was called the Blue Topped Cabins. The cabins looked old and run-down. A remnant from the fifties. Olivia at this place? Not a chance.

She entered the lobby and spotted an old man sitting behind the desk. At first she couldn't figure out what the thin, black streak was that ran down one side of his chin. She wrinkled her nose. Ugh. Tobacco juice.

He pushed himself up from his chair. "What can I do for you?"

"I'd like to show you a photo and see if this person stayed here recently."

He fumbled around for a pair of wire-rimmed glasses and studied the picture. "Yep, I seen her."

Rachel stepped closer to the desk. "You did? When?"

He scratched the two-day growth on his chin. "About a week ago. She was in here with a whole group of girls. All from downstate." He handed the picture back. "A bunch of rowdies they were, let me tell you. Had to toss 'em outta here because of all their racket. They was disturbing all the other guests."

Rachel tried not to let him see how disappointed she was. She held up the picture again. "Could you look once more? Are you sure it was her?"

He took off his glasses, wiped them with his shirttail, and put them back on. "Oh, yeah. That's her all right."

She took back the picture. "Okay. Well, thank you for your time."

She returned to her car. She was cold, wet, and had run out of places to check. Clearly the old man was wrong. Olivia hadn't come up here with a bunch of girls from downstate. If only she had.

Rachel pounded the steering wheel. Where had they stayed? How was it possible nobody recognized her? Should she start looking at campgrounds? There was no way Olivia would have put up with sleeping in a tent. What else was left? She'd checked every place in the phone book.

There was a buzzing from her purse. She pulled her cellphone out and saw it was her mother calling. What to say? Tell her she'd hit a dead end? "Hi, Mom."

"Rachel! I can't believe I got through to you."

"Me either. The reception around here is awful. I'm sitting on top of a mountain. That must be why."

"Have you found out anything?"

"No, but I've still got a few more places to check out," she lied.

"I wanted to tell you, I found a picture on my phone that Olivia sent me. I think you should see it."

"You've got a picture? A picture of what?"

Her mother explained that she had been going through her messages and found a picture of an old barn Olivia had sent the first day of their trip.

"Send it to me. Maybe I can find someone who knows where it is."

They talked for a few more minutes and then hung up. A few seconds later, her phone pinged. There it was. An old barn that looked like it was about to tumble over. Why had Olivia taken a picture of it? How was that going to help? They certainly didn't stay in a barn. She fought back tears and started the car. It was raining again.

When she pulled into town, Rachel spotted another bar. Perfect. She needed a drink. She ran from the car as fast as she could, but by the time she got inside, she was soaked.

"Nasty out there, isn't it? What can I get you?" The bartender grabbed a bar towel and handed it to her.

She wiped her face. "Thanks. I'll have a beer. Do you serve lunch?"

"We sure do. Let me get you a menu." He got her beer and then handed her a menu. "Supposed to rain all day. What brings you out in this kind of weather?"

Rachel leaned forward and attempted to dry her hair with the towel. She tried not to cry, but tears streamed down her face. She turned away.

"Is something wrong?"

She pressed the towel against her eyes, wishing the tears would stop. "No, I'll be all right." She took a breath and reached into her purse for Olivia's picture. "Have you seen her?"

"I sure have."

Rachel looked up. "You have? You've seen her?" She held her breath. Please, not another case of mistaken identity.

"Yeah. Twice. The first time she was with her creepy boyfriend who almost got in a fight with me the other night over at Sudsy's. Then the next day he showed up here. He picked a fight with a friend of mine and almost killed him. The poor guy's lying on the floor bleeding, and they just take off. That guy's a real jerk." He offered his hand. "By the way, the name's Paul."

"I'm Rachel." She looked down at the photograph. "Olivia's sister." She leaned closer. "When was that? When were they here?"

Paul thought for a moment. "It was last week. Friday? No, it wasn't Friday. Let me think. Yes, it was the night before. Thursday. They were in here Thursday."

"They didn't happen to mention where they were staying, did they?"

"No, why? What's going on?"

"She never came home. I'm trying to figure out what happened. I've checked out every single motel around here, but nobody's seen her." She remembered the picture her mother sent. She pulled out her phone. "How about this? Have you ever seen this old barn?"

Paul leaned over the bar. "Not that I can remember, but there's probably a hundred of those around here." He looked back at her. "Why the barn?"

"My sister sent this to my mother the first day they got here. I have no idea why. Probably because it looked cool to her or something. I thought if I found out where it is, at least it would give me some place to start looking."

Paul poured himself a soft drink. "I sure hope nothing's happened to her. Can I ask you a question?"

"Sure."

"Your sister seemed like a real nice girl. What was she doing with that nutcase?"

Rachel sighed. "I don't know. I never met him, but I've talked to a few of her girlfriends. They didn't like him either. I really don't know how much she knew about him. They hadn't been going out for very long."

"He seemed like he was walking around with a permanent chip on his shoulder."

"He was a rebound for her. Her fiancé got killed in Afghanistan a year ago. She took it real hard. I think this is the first guy she's dated since."

"The punk claimed he was an ex-Marine. He sure didn't act like one." Paul got Rachel another beer. "Here. This one's on the house."

"Thank you."

"Where have you been looking?"

She pulled out her paper and read off all of the places she'd been.

Paul drummed his fingers on the bar. "I'm trying to think if you missed any place. We're in the middle of nowhere up here. There aren't that many places to stay. What about campgrounds? We've got our share of those."

Rachel shook her head. "No, that would be the last place she would stay. Believe me, I'm sure about that. I talked with a woman at the visitor's center. She saw them too. So I know they got here. And now you saw them. I just wonder where they decided to sleep." She picked up the menu. "I'm starving. Any recommendations?"

"We're known for our Italian cuisine. We use the owner's old family recipes. I'd recommend the manicotti. Our meatball subs are great too."

She thought for a moment. "I'll have the sub."

Paul put the order in and walked to the end of the bar to take care of two other customers.

After Rachel got her lunch, she ordered another drink. A few more people had come in, and the bartender was busy with them. She looked out the window. It was still raining. She had run out of ideas. Again, tears came. She needed to get back to the motel. Maybe a nap would make her feel better. Hopefully, she could come up with another plan.

Olivia lay on the bed and stared into the darkness. She was hungry and her throat was dry. How long could a person go without water? She knew it was a lot less time than going without food.

He must have meant it when he said he wasn't going to bring her anything else to eat. How long had it been? From the tiny sliver of light that seeped through the small crack in the plywood, it must have been Tuesday evening? Or was it Wednesday?

She pulled the blanket over her head. Maybe she wouldn't be so thirsty if she could fall asleep.

Arnold sat at the kitchen table by the window and ate a bowl of soup. Raindrops dripped off the eaves of the house. As he took a sip of Mountain Dew, the phone rang. He jumped. Oh, no. Not another pissed off vacationer wanting to give him hell for canceling their reservation. He picked up the receiver.

"Hello, Arnold. It's Mr. Jacobson. I'd like to speak to your mother, please."

Arnold gripped the receiver tighter. "I told you Mother's too sick to take your calls."

"Listen, I know something's going on over there, and I'm going to get to the bottom of it. I've asked you nicely several times to have your mother call me back, and it never happens. I asked you if she was in the hospital, and you said no. I tell you what. I'll give you twenty-four hours to have your mother call me. If I haven't heard from her by then, I'll be paying you a visit with the sheriff alongside me. We'll conduct a wellness check on her. You got that? Twenty-four hours."

Arnold yanked the receiver from his ear as Mr. Jacobson slammed down the phone. Arnold paced the kitchen. He needed a plan. What could he come up with? Mr. Jacobson was becoming a pain in the ass. Nobody else gave a damn about his mother. Only that sex pervert. What could he tell him to make him back off?

He finished his lunch and looked at the clock. Almost one o'clock. Should he bring something down for that girl? No, let her go a little longer. She had to learn that there were consequences for not going along with his plan.

He glanced down at his arm. The sling had been a good idea. That and the Advil he'd been taking dulled the pain. Should he drive to the emergency room in Houghton? No, there was no money for any hospital visit.

Arnold picked up his bowl and walked over to the sink. He stopped at the kitchen window. A doe and two fawns stood in the backyard. His father used to put out a salt lick and stand on the back porch with his deer rifle. It had been years since they had a salt lick, but the deer kept coming just the same. He rinsed out his bowl. Wait a minute. Mr. Jacobson. That was it!

Arnold went over to a piece of paper his mother had taped to the wall near the phone. He found Mr. Jacobson's number and dialed it. "This is Arnold. I've just talked to Mother. She tells me she's feeling better and would like to see you this evening. When? She said around eight-thirty. You can? Okay. See you then." He hung up. Problem solved.

Arnold went into his father's closet and pulled out the deer rifle. He found a box of shells on a top shelf. He'd shot the rifle many times, mostly target practice shooting cans in the backyard, but he had gone hunting only once. It had been a disaster.

He and his father went back in the woods behind the house where they followed the many deer trails that meandered back there. They sat on a ridge and waited. It hadn't been long until a doe wandered down the trail. His father nodded for Arnold to shoot. He aimed and slowly squeezed the trigger like his father had taught him. The shot connected, but it wasn't good. The deer didn't drop. It let out a scream, stumbled, and then ran down the path bleeding.

His father grabbed the gun from him and chased after the deer. It wasn't hard to find. Just follow the blood trail. Arnold was there when his father finished it off. They gutted it out on the trail. That's when they saw the fawns. Two spotted fawns were watching them. He never went hunting again. Those damn dreams. It had taken years for them to stop.

Arnold grabbed the gun and walked back to the kitchen. That hunting trip seemed like it happened a hundred years ago.

After dinner and a little TV, Arnold took the rifle and positioned himself behind a clump of fir trees near the garage. He wished he'd told Mr. Jacobson to come later because it wouldn't be dark until after ten o'clock. He took a practice aim at the front porch. Damn summer. If this was December, it would have been dark by five-thirty.

Gravel crunched at the far end of the driveway. Arnold stepped back and disappeared into the trees. There he was. Good old Mr. Jacobson. Right on time. He was about to get screwed, all right. But this time it would be on Arnold's terms.

Mr. Jacobson got out of the car and walked toward the front porch. He whistled as he reached into his back pocket and pulled out a comb.

Arnold quietly stepped out of the woods and rested the barrel of the rifle on the hood of his car. Just as he was about to squeeze the trigger, Mr. Jacobson turned.

"Arnold! What the hell are you——."

A shot rang out and Mr. Jacobson fell to the ground just inches in front of the porch. This time it was a kill shot. Right below the shoulders and through the heart.

Arnold waited to be sure Mr. Jacobson wasn't moving. Then Arnold got into his car and slowly backed up next to the body. He unloaded a long chain from the trunk and wrapped it around Mr. Jacobson's legs.

It was much easier pulling this corpse out behind the barn. No more getting that girl involved and putting up with her nonsense. He stopped the car next to the barn, undid the chain, and rolled Mr. Jacobson into some tall weeds next to his mother. He'd have to figure out what to do with the bodies in the morning. There was no way he was going to be able to dig a grave. His arm was already aching. Why hadn't he brought his sling along? Tomorrow he would drive Mr. Jacobson's truck into the forest down the old woods road that ended at the swamp. It would be hidden deep in the woods right in the middle of their twenty-acre property. Maybe he'd push it into the muddy water. Didn't matter. Nobody would ever find it.

Chapter 13

RACHEL CHECKED THE motel room for the second time to make sure she hadn't missed anything. She grabbed her suitcase and headed down to her car. She hoped they wouldn't charge her a late fee. It was almost noon, and checkout was at ten-thirty.

As she drove toward town, she wondered if that bartender was working at Russo's Tavern. She had only had two cups of coffee from the little pot in her room. Having missed breakfast, she was hungry. Rachel parked in front of the bar. When she stepped inside, she was happy to see Paul was working.

He waved. "Any news on your sister?"

She shook her head. A sudden sadness overtook her. "I haven't found out anything except that they were here. Nobody was able to tell me anything except you and the lady over at the park." She reached into her purse for a tissue. "What am I going to tell Mother? That Olivia just disappeared, and I came home with nothing?" She dabbed her eyes.

"Have you filed a missing person's report?"

She shook her head. "Not yet. I'm still hanging on to hope that they were having such a great time, they decided to stay a little longer."

Paul leaned closer. "I don't know about that. Maybe it's something you should think about." He thought for a moment. "Why are you going home?"

She looked up. "I've done everything I can think of. I have no new ideas. And…I'm almost out of money. I couldn't stay in the motel anymore."

"That's no reason to leave," Paul said. "There has to be something you haven't thought of."

"I'm sure there is," Rachel said. "But even if I thought of something new, I don't really want to start sleeping in my car."

"You want a drink?" Paul asked. "It's on the house."

"Well, if you're buying…sure. Give me a beer."

As Paul got her drink, Rachel grabbed a menu. "Can I get a slice of pizza? I'll pay for that."

Paul handed her the beer. "Sure." He wrote her selection on a slip and took it back to the kitchen. When he returned, he said, "I've got an idea."

"What?"

"Why don't you stay a few more days? Tell me what you've done so far and anything else you can think of about your sister and that creepy boyfriend of hers. You can stay at my place. It's not much. Just a typical bachelor pad, but it's better than going back and telling your mother you hit a dead-end."

Rachel sat back. "Ah, well, that's awfully nice of you, but—"

Paul smiled. "I know. You don't know anything about me. I'll give you a quick bio. Had a few girlfriends, but I've

114

never been married. Did four years in the Marines right after high school. I'm working on my bachelor's degree."

Rachel laughed. "You're the one who should be worried. You don't know anything about me. And I'm not about to start explaining my checkered past."

Paul grabbed a phone from under the bar and dialed a number. As it was ringing, he said, "My friend's a bigwig up at the park. I want to ask him something." He winked. "And he can give you a personal reference that I'm not an axe murderer."

Paul waited another few seconds. "Charlie, Paul here. Hey, I wanted to run something by you. Remember that girl who was in here with her nasty boyfriend? The guy that dragged her outside. Well, her sister's here looking for her. Seems she didn't get home when she was supposed to. I wondered if anyone up there found a vehicle parked at a trailhead overnight or anything like that." He listened. "No? Okay. I guess that's a good thing. Oh, can you do me a favor? I need you to talk to her sister. Her name's Rachel. Tell her what a great guy I am." He handed the phone to her.

Before she took it, she asked, "Tommy dragged her out of here?"

Paul nodded. "I'll explain everything after the call."

Rachel took the phone and listened for a few minutes. Suddenly she burst out laughing and handed the receiver back to Paul.

He said goodbye and hung up. "What was so funny?"

"I can't tell you. But I guess it'll be okay if I accept your offer, if you don't mind."

The waitress brought Rachel her pizza.

"That damn Charlie. I can only imagine what he said." Paul checked on a few other customers and then returned.

"Okay. Why don't you tell me everything you can about what you've done and what I should know about your sister."

"I will, but first you have to tell me about Tommy dragging Olivia."

Arnold looked up the forestry service number and dialed the phone. "I need a burning permit for 156 Turner Lane."

The clerk commented on how wet it had been and then wrote up the paperwork. He gave the permit number to Arnold and asked, "When do you expect to do the burning?""

"I've got some old lumber and trash I'd like to get rid of. Probably in about an hour, if that's okay."

"Not a problem. Thank you for calling this in. It saves us a lot of time and manpower when we don't have to chase down unauthorized fires. Have a nice day."

Arnold hung up. There was one more thing. He went down to his room in the basement and picked up the trunk with the pretty clothes his mother used to make him dress up in.

He carried it out the back door over to where the bodies were lying in the tall grass. He went to the old barn and retrieved a gas can he used for the riding mower. He had already rolled Mr. Jacobson's body closer to his mother. He poured gasoline over both of them and then piled pieces of old lumber from the barn over the corpses, along with the trunk.

Arnold stood back, lit an oily rag, and tossed it on the pile. A huge orange flame shot skyward. A blast of hot air knocked him backward. Flames shot high into the air. The fire was much larger than he had anticipated. Burning embers rode heat waves up into the sky and landed hundreds of feet away in the meadow. Another shower of sparks floated upward. Thank goodness the recent rains had kept the ground moist.

A plume of white smoke erupted from the barn roof. Glowing embers swirled in the wind and landed on the structure's wooden shingles. Unlike the ground, the old roof was dried out from the sun. Small flames ran along the ridge line. Arnold stepped back, his eyes wide. Shit, the whole damn thing was about to go up in flames. The barn was packed with stuff. He ran inside and frantically looked around. What to grab first?

He jumped on the riding mower and drove it out to the middle of the field. He ran back hoping to find a garden hose. By the time he returned, the whole north side of the barn was on fire. Dark clouds of black smoke billowed skyward.

Would all this smoke be enough to bring out the firetrucks, or would his permit keep the authorities at bay? He ran over to where he'd started the fire. It was still going strong. The flames and ash from the lumber made it impossible to make out anything in the rubble. That was good. What would be left after the fire was out?

Arnold paced back and forth straining to hear the sounds of sirens in the distance. A shrill ringing made him jump. The phone. Who was calling him now? He needed to adjust that stupid outside ringer. It was enough to wake the...whatever.

He ran back to the house and grabbed the receiver. "No, everything's under control. Yes, it was a little larger than I had anticipated. I've been cleaning up around the area, and I had a big pile of brush to burn along with some old timber. Thank you for checking. I've got things under control. Good-bye." He leaned against the kitchen door and caught his breath. Thank God he'd called in to get that permit.

Duck was hunched over the desk examining a broken clasp through his eye loop when Juliette walked in. He pushed the loop up. "Is it noon already?"

She laughed. "No, it's only ten-thirty. I wanted to see you." She pulled a chair close and lowered her voice. "Dieter is gone doing an errand."

"What's he got against me? He seems to always get mad when he sees me talking to you."

She waved her hand. "He's a big baby. We...we used to...you know, be a couple, but it didn't work out. He was a boxer over in Germany. I think he took too many—" She paused and then made a fist and punched the air. "How do you say it in English?"

"Blows? Hits to the head?"

"*Oui.* That is what I am trying to say. He is a nice man, but there are some problems." She thought for a moment. "*Monsieur* Duck, it's hard for us to meet people because Mrs. Haverhill always wants us to be here for her. And then we move around so much. From one house to another." She reached out and took his hand. "But don't worry about Dieter. He does not own me."

Her hands were soft. Duck reveled in her perfume. "I've got an idea. How about I take you out to dinner tonight?"

Juliette shook her head. "I have to cook for Mrs. Haverhill." She thought for a moment. "But I could meet you later on, say about nine?"

"Okay. How about Russo's Tavern? It's right on Main Street. You can't miss it."

She stood up. "I will see you tonight."

Duck watched as she exited the room. Was it his imagination, or was her bottom swaying a little more than usual?

He turned back to his work. How was he supposed to concentrate now?

Olivia sat on the mattress in complete darkness. She shivered from the cold dampness of the room. From the other side of the door, the scraping of the bolt as it slid open made Olivia push herself back into the corner. The lights snapped on. She covered her eyes from the brightness as the door swung open.

She slid even tighter against the wall and waited for her eyes to adjust. A delicious smell permeated the room. Olivia tried to control herself. She didn't want to give him the satisfaction of knowing how hungry and thirsty she was.

Arnold stepped inside and set a tray down on the floor. "Here you go. This is for you. I picked up some Italian food for us. It's from a place everyone around here goes to for their great cooking."

She remained pressed against the wall.

"Well, come on. I've got two orders of lasagna, some garlic bread, two salads, and some wine." He tossed her a bottle of water. "Here. You can probably use this too."

The bottle hit the wall and fell next to her. She grabbed it, twisted off the cap, and forced herself to drink slowly. When the bottle was empty, she took her plate of food and began to eat.

"It's kind of quiet upstairs now. You know, with Mother gone. I'd really like the time to come when you get tired of it down here, and you could move upstairs." He noticed the empty water bottle. "Let me get you some more. We've got a utility sink down here." He took her bottle and stepped out of the coal bin. He walked backwards toward the sink, keeping an eye on the open door.

He quickly filled the bottle and returned. "Here. You see, that was good. I got you some water, and you didn't try anything stupid."

She ate steadily, trying not to show him how hungry she was. She noticed Arnold had a spot of red sauce on his chin.

All through the meal, Olivia felt as if Arnold had something he wanted to tell her. Finally, when his plate was empty, he asked, "How about that book I left? Did you read it?"

She turned and stared at him. Was he a complete idiot? "Ah, the lights were off. Do you know how dark it is down here when the lights are off?"

Arnold's face flushed. He pulled a white garbage bag out of his back pocket and gathered up the paper plates and plastic utensils. He grabbed the plastic bucket and stepped out into the basement. This time he closed the door and swiveled the sturdy two-by four down into the metal cradle.

After emptying the bucket in the toilet upstairs, he returned to the coal bin door. He lifted the homemade locking mechanism, pulled open the door, and set the bucket inside. "I'll leave the lights on this time. Maybe you can start reading that book."

It was five o'clock in the afternoon when Rachel entered Paul's apartment. She had stayed at Russo's all afternoon. She enjoyed talking with Paul. He seemed truly interested in helping her find out about her sister. She looked around. It wasn't a typical bachelor pad like he had said. It seemed much cleaner than most men's places she had seen. Probably due to his time in the Marines.

She entered the kitchen. A stack of clean dishes was sitting in the drying rack next to the sink.

Rachel returned to the living room, clicked on the television, and sat on the couch. She was tired. Too many drinks. She needed a nap. Paul wanted her to return to the bar around eight o'clock. She set her cellphone alarm and pulled a blanket off the back of the couch. This was much better than staying in a motel room by herself.

A ringing telephone jolted her awake. She sat up and tried to find where the sound was coming from. It was in the kitchen. She threw off the blanket and ran to answer it. "Hello."

It was Paul. "I thought you were coming back to the bar?"

"What time is it?"

"It's almost nine-thirty."

"What?" She glanced around the kitchen for a clock. "I'm sorry, Paul. I lay down on the couch and fell asleep. I'll be right there."

Half an hour later, she entered Russo's. Paul was talking to a couple at the other end of the bar. She took a seat and waited for him to come over.

"Hello, sleepyhead. Did you have a nice beauty rest?"

She smiled. "I can't believe I did that. I set an alarm on my phone but slept right through it."

"You must have needed the rest. How was the apartment?"

"Very clean. You must be some kind of neat freak."

"I try my best. Hey, I'd like you to meet a friend of mine." He took her over to the couple he had been talking with when she walked in. "This is Duck Lindquist and his friend Juliette."

Duck nodded as Juliette said, "*Bonjour*."

"Duck's the guy your sister's boyfriend beat up," Paul said.

Rachel's eyes widened. "You met my sister?"

Duck frowned. "Well, kind of. I—" He glanced over at Juliette. "I had a few beers, and I was on my way to the restroom. I walked by your sister on the way and did something that made her boyfriend crazy."

Rachel pulled the photograph out of her purse. "Is this who you saw?"

Duck nodded. "That's her all right."

As Rachel was putting the picture away, Juliette asked, "Can I see it, please?"

Rachel handed it to her.

"She's very pretty."

"And very missing," Rachel said. "I sure wish I could figure out where she is."

"Show Duck that barn picture," Paul said. "He's lived here almost all his life. Maybe he'll recognize it."

Rachel pulled out her phone and scrolled to the picture. She handed it to Duck. "Olivia sent this to our mother the first day she arrived. I don't know if it would help or not, but I'd like to figure out where it was taken."

Duck and Juliette both stared at the screen. Duck said, "I don't know. I've seen a lot of old barns around here, and this one doesn't stand out. But if you look over to the right, where the field is, you can see water. Looks like it's somewhere on the Lake Superior shoreline."

Paul moved over so he could see the picture again. "Yeah, you're right. I never noticed that before. That eliminates a lot of territory."

Duck handed the phone back to Rachel. "But it may not have been taken around here. They could have spotted it on the way and just pulled over to take the shot."

"I think maybe that is what happened," Juliette said. "No one would be staying at such a place."

Rachel sighed. She's probably right. Her barn picture was probably more wishful thinking than an actual clue. "I love your accent, Juliette. Where are you from?"

Juliette explained that she was born and raised in a town about six hours south of Paris, but she moved to the United States two years ago to work for Mrs. Haverhill.

Duck told Rachel about the magnificent French chateaux and the history of the Haverhill mine, how instrumental it had been for the growth of the area, and how most mining in the county was now shut down.

Paul turned to Juliette. "I was surprised when Duck told me he got a job at the Haverhill mansion. I thought it was all boarded up and wasn't being used."

"*Oui*, it has been vacant. We've been coming here for the last two years. We arrive early in May and usually leave the second week in October. Mrs. Haverhill used to come here with her husband when they first got married. It has many nice memories for her. But you are correct. The place was not used for many years. It took her a long time to get it fixed."

Around midnight Juliette told Duck she had better be getting back. After everyone said their goodbyes, Paul announced it was last call to the rest of the patrons. Half an hour later, he closed up the bar and followed Rachel back to his apartment.

When they arrived, Paul said, "You sleep in my bed. I'll sleep on the couch tonight."

"Are you crazy?" I'm not taking your bed. I slept just fine on the couch this afternoon."

"No, I insist. You can shut and lock the door, and you won't have to worry about anything."

"Lock the door? You've listened to me tell my sad story about my sister. You're kind enough to let me stay here." She sat down on the couch.

Paul took some sheets, a pillow, and a blanket from a hall closet and set them on an end table. "See. I'll be just fine here tonight." He turned to her. "You want a nightcap?"

"Sure."

Paul got her a beer and opened a Coke for himself.

"You're not drinking?" Rachel asked.

"I quit about a year ago."

She laughed. "You're a bartender. Why?"

"Let's just say I've had my share. Anyway, I've been thinking. It sounds like Duck and I were the last people to see your sister. After she walked out of the bar, nobody's seen her since."

Rachel sat deep in thought.

After a few minutes Paul asked, "What are you thinking about?"

"Olivia. Why would she take a trip with that guy? He sounds terrible. I don't know if I told you, but her fiancé was killed in Afghanistan about a year ago. I didn't like him much, but he was a saint compared to Tommy."

"Oh, I'm sorry to hear that. Why didn't you like her fiancé?"

"He didn't treat her very well. He was bossy and self-centered."

"It seems like your sister is attracted to the wrong kind of man."

Rachel frowned. "Yeah, it runs in our family."

Paul's eyebrows shot up. "Oh, really. Tell me more."

She shook her head. "No, I'm here on a mission, and talking about myself isn't going to get anything accomplished. When I heard what you told me about Tommy, I couldn't imagine how she could have gotten tied up with that guy."

"He probably put on a great front. She thought she was going to have a fun getaway and then his real colors came out."

Rachel took a sip of her beer. "After what you and Duck told me about that horrible fight he had with Duck, there's no way she'd stay with him after that."

Paul nodded. "That's what I was thinking. But where would she go? It was late. They were in his car. They roll up the streets around here about eight o'clock. Where would she have gone? The closest bus depot is forty miles away." Paul opened his soda. "Do you think she may have jumped out of his car and started hitchhiking?"

"No, Olivia would never hitchhike. I'm sure of that."

Paul yawned. "Excuse me. It's been a long day. I pulled a double shift."

Rachel grabbed his hand, stood up, and pulled him to his feet. She shoved him toward the bedroom door. "Go. Get in there and get some sleep."

He resisted. "No, I told you, you could—"

She wrapped her arms around him and kissed him. "You've been so good to me. Go to bed now. I'm going to finish my beer, think about my sister, and sleep just fine on the couch. How about if I make you breakfast in the morning?"

Paul stepped back, a little surprised. "Ah, that sounds great."

125

When he left the room, Rachel sat back down on the couch. She smiled. Amazing. She had finally met a great guy. She was staying in his apartment, but the guy was a complete teetotaler.

She finished her beer, spread the sheets out on the couch, and lay down. Maybe he'd find some reason not to spend all night in that bedroom by himself.

Chapter 14

OLIVIA TOSSED THE book aside. This guy was totally crazy. Science fiction? What kind of planet was run totally by men who kept women in cages for the sole purpose of breeding?

She stood up and walked around the small room. There had to be a way out. She pushed on the sheets of plywood that covered some kind of opening for the hundredth time. They didn't budge.

This wasn't going to end well. He would either rape her or kill her. Probably both. She needed some kind of weapon. If she could attack him somehow when he came in the door, she could run out and find a way to get back home. How was her mother doing? What about Rachel? Was she coming over to help, or was she leaving everything for poor Elaine?

Olivia looked around. What could she use as a weapon? The bucket? No, it was plastic. Too bad he had removed the wire handle. If it was still there, she could poke him in the eye or something. Maybe she could throw the blanket over him when he came in. But then what?

As she flopped back down, a scraping sound came from underneath the mattress. What was that? She kneeled on the floor, stuck her hand under the mattress, and pulled out a plastic spoon. It must have come from the milkshake that dumped over. Too bad it hadn't been a knife. A nice long hunting knife with a sharp edge. That was what she needed. She shoved the spoon back where she found it.

What time was it? She went over to the plywood boards and moved the chair to where the small crack was. She stood on the chair and pressed her eye close to the opening. There was only darkness.

Arnold paced the living room. Why wasn't he happy? Those damn girly clothes were all burned up. His mother was gone, and he had the house all to himself. But somehow, he didn't feel alone. Every time he walked by his mother's room, it was like she was still there.

Her clothes were all there. Her perfume was still there. Everything was still there but Mother. He swore he had heard her voice calling out his name.

He was tired. He wasn't sleeping well. He had started sleeping upstairs. Not in Olivia's room, but in the other guest room. He didn't like staying in the basement anymore. Too close to the coal bin.

He thought about Leslie. Her hair. How pretty she was. The smug look on her face when she embarrassed him in front of everybody at school. She should be down in the coal bin. Then they could be together. He could do things to her. Make her sorry for how she treated him. Well, guess what. Leslie wasn't in the basement, was she? Someone else was.

There was a noise at the door. Olivia jumped off the chair and pushed it back to where it had been. She sat down on the mattress.

The door swung open and Arnold walked in. He looked tense. He was sweating. He pulled the teddy out of his back pocket and tossed it near her. He had a knife in his other hand. "Take off your clothes and put that on."

She pressed herself farther into the corner. He looked like a different person. "I…I read some of your book."

He stepped closer and thrust the knife near her. "Shut up. Get undressed."

She slowly unbuttoned her blouse and slid it off her shoulder. It fluttered down onto the mattress.

"Keep going."

She reached back and undid her bra.

He moved the knife to his left hand and cupped her breast.

Tears ran down her face. This was it. His hand left her breast.

He unzipped his pants. Arnold backed away. Rivulets of sweat ran down the sides of his face. His hair was plastered to his head. "I…I can't—"

He spun around and stumbled out of the room. The door slammed shut behind him.

Olivia grabbed her blouse and wrapped it around her shoulders. She wanted to cry but couldn't. She bowed her head. *Please, God. Let me find a way out of here.*

Rachel was making pancakes when Paul came out of the bedroom. He yawned. "I smell coffee."

"Breakfast will be ready in a few minutes."

He poured himself a cup. "I've got an idea for today."

Rachel flipped a pancake. "You do? What is it?"

"I thought we'd drive around some of the old roads here and look for that barn you showed me."

She turned from the stove. "What about work?"

"I pulled a double shift yesterday. I'm off today."

She loaded up a plate with pancakes and set them on the table. "Thank you. I'd really like that."

Paul took a bite. "Hmm. These are good. Thanks for making breakfast." He took a sip of coffee. "I know you've been trying to find where your sister stayed up here, but what do you know about this boyfriend of hers?"

Rachel shook her head. "Not much. Actually, almost nothing. All I know is his name is Tommy Riggins, and he's from Lansing."

Paul's eyebrows shot up. "That's it?"

She shrugged. "Olivia and I weren't that close. She was off to college. That's where she met him."

"We need to get his phone number and give him a call."

"I have it. I've called several times, but nobody answers.

"Why don't you try it again?"

She excused herself and went into the bedroom. Fifteen minutes later she returned to the table.

"How'd you do?"

"I called the number and got his mother. I told her who I was and said I wanted to talk to Tommy. She told me he wasn't there. Took a bus to New York City. I asked her if he said anything about his trip to the Porcupine Mountains. His mother said he didn't have a good time. Things didn't work out with his girlfriend, and he needed to get away. He was staying with an old Marine buddy in New York City."

"Did you tell her your sister was missing?"

Rachel nodded. "I did. At the end of the call. That seemed to make her want to get off the phone. She muttered something about Tommy not having any luck with women and then hung up."

Paul thought for a minute. "That's odd. Have you reported her missing to the police?"

"Not yet. I wanted to come up here first. That seemed so, you know, final. I was desperately hoping I'd find her here, and she'd be fine. Just staying a few days longer with her new boyfriend."

"On our way out of town, we're going to stop at the sheriff's office so you can file a report."

Rachel put her cup down. "Okay."

Duck was bent over the desk carefully soldering a broken clasp onto a long necklace when Juliette came into the room holding two cups of coffee. He looked up. "Well, now. This is a treat."

She set the cups down on his worktable and pulled over a chair. "A little surprise for you." She smiled and leaned toward him.

As he reached for his coffee, Duck paused. Instead of the sedate black blouse buttoned to the neck that Juliette normally wore, she was now wearing a shear pink top which presented him with an unrestricted view of her abundant cleavage. He smiled. Was the surprise the coffee or the view? "Ah, thank you."

"I had a very nice time last night, *Monsieur* Duck. It was nice to meet your friends."

"I had a great time too. I'm so glad you were able to get away." Duck glanced toward the doorway.

"You don't have to worry. Dieter is in town buying food, and Mrs. Haverhill is upstairs." She stood up, pulled Duck to his feet, and wrapped her arms around him.

As her warm body pressed into his, he pulled her closer and kissed her.

131

After several moments, she broke from the embrace and pulled him toward the library. "This way. We can have more…privacy."

Paul's car traveled down a narrow road that wound its way through the dense woodland.

"How do you know where you're going?" Rachel asked.

As the car bounced over a muddy rut, Rachel grabbed the door handle to steady herself.

"When I was sixteen, I made a car out of an old fifty-six Chevy to drive around the woods. It didn't have any doors or top. We used to take it down all of these old logging trails." He pulled up to a field and cut the engine. "Come on. I want to show you something."

Rachel followed him down a narrow path to the top of a tall sand dune.

Paul pointed. "How about that view?"

Rachel stared in amazement. "It's beautiful. How high up are we? It looks like it's a long way down to the water."

"I'd say it's about five hundred feet. We could easily run down the sand all the way to the shoreline, but it would probably take two hours for us to climb back up."

"I'll pass," she said.

"Turn around."

Rachel turned. Between the trees an old barn stood in the middle of a clearing.

Paul grinned. "I hope this is the barn we're looking for."

She pulled out her phone and found the picture. "I don't think it's the same one." She handed the phone to him.

"Damn. I was sure this was it. I didn't remember it when you showed me the picture at the bar. But I knew I had seen one like it somewhere. It came to me this morning. That's why

I wanted to bring you here." He glanced at the photo again. "You're right. It's not the same. But don't worry. I've got a few more roads we can check out."

They got back into the car, and Paul started down the narrow road. "I don't know about you, but I wasn't very happy with our trip to the sheriff's office."

Rachel turned to him. "No kidding. Once he heard Olivia was up here with her boyfriend, he didn't seem to be very interested. He said to check back in a few days."

"I know. I tried to stress the urgency of this, but I guess they're too wrapped up with that body they found up on the mountain."

Rachel grabbed his arm. "Oh, I never told you. The desk clerk at my motel came up to the room and told me to turn on the television. I watched a news report about that poor girl and almost died. For a few minutes I thought they were talking about Olivia. Then they said the date when they found her. Olivia hadn't even left the house yet." She clenched his arm. "I thought I was going to faint."

"That must have been awful. Thank goodness it wasn't her."

Paul drove to two other locations, but each one had a different barn than the one in the picture. He pulled onto Greenland Road. "Let's stop in at Russo's and have lunch."

"Okay. I'm going to give Mother a quick call. I hope I have service."

"We're in town. Shouldn't be a problem here."

She pulled out her cellphone. "Great. I've got three bars." She scrolled down to the number. "Mom? Hi, it's Rachel. Yes, I'm fine. No, I haven't found her yet. I've gone to some of the motels around here, but I have a few more to check out."

There was a long silence. "I don't know where she could be, but I'm not finished looking. Oh, I went to the police and reported her missing. They'll be looking for her too. How are you? You don't sound so good." Rachel listened. "I woke you? I'm sorry. I know, Mom. So do I. Look, I need to run. I'll call you again soon. Okay?"

Paul pulled into the parking lot. "How's your mom?"

Rachel fought back tears. "She sounded weak. I wish I had better news."

He pulled her close. "You're doing all you can."

When they walked into the tavern, Paul saw Duck sitting at the bar by himself.

Duck turned. "There you are. I turned down a free lunch because I needed to show you something. I'm supposed to be fixing jewelry. I was just about to leave, but I wanted you to see this."

"See what?" Paul smiled. "If it's a ring from the estate, I'm not really in the market."

Duck didn't laugh. He tossed a newspaper onto the bar and then noticed Rachel. "Oh. Sorry. I…I didn't know you had company."

Paul pulled out a bar stool for Rachel and sat down next to Duck. "You know Rachel."

Duck nodded. "Hello."

"We were driving around trying to find that old barn she showed us last night." Paul waved to the bartender. "Hi, Marty. Everything okay?"

"Yeah. Not too busy. Can I get you guys anything?"

Rachel ordered a beer.

Paul turned back to Duck. "You said you wanted me to see something."

Duck took a deep breath. "Take a look at this." He turned over the paper.

Paul studied the front page. "Okay. They did a reconstruction on that skull they found near Summit Peak." He looked up at Duck. "And?"

"Look again. Does she look like anyone you know?"

Paul pulled the paper closer and studied the picture. "What are you trying to say? You think it looks like Grace?"

Rachel turned. "Grace? Who's Grace?"

"I sure as shit do!" Duck said. "And I'm not the only one." He tapped the picture with his finger. "You don't think so?"

Paul looked up at Rachel. "My old girlfriend."

Rachel grabbed him. "Are you telling me the skull they found on the mountain looks like your old girlfriend?"

Paul stared at the picture again. "It does." He turned to Duck. "Well, it resembles her, I guess. But so what? It can't be Grace. The last I heard, she was living in Chicago. This...this is just a reconstruction. It's not like some kind of photograph or something."

"Why don't you call her," Rachel said, "and find out if she's all right?"

Paul sat back. "Call her? Oh, I don't think so. We didn't part on the best of terms. I have no idea where she is in Chicago." He pointed to the paper. "Just because there's some resemblance doesn't mean it's her. I'm telling you, it's not her."

Marty walked over holding a phone. "Charlie wants to talk to you."

Paul took the receiver. "Not you too! Jeez. I'm down here with Rachel and Duck. I just saw the paper. Duck showed me. Yes, it does look like Grace. I know. I know. Okay, I'll see you later." He handed the phone back to Marty.

"Maybe you better call Grace," Duck said. "I don't think this is going away anytime soon."

Chapter 15

A LOUD KNOCKING woke Rachel. She felt Paul lying next to her in bed. They had stayed up late the night before talking. She had taken him by the hand and led him into the bedroom. It had been wonderful. Something nice to take her mind off everything else.

She gently shook him. "Paul, someone's at the front door."

He stirred and moved closer to her.

She shook him again. "Hey, wake up. Someone's here."

He blinked a few times, and when he saw she was in bed next to him, he smiled. He grabbed her. "Come over here, baby."

She gave him a shove. "Not now! Someone's at the door."

He rolled over and looked at the clock. "Shit. It's almost nine." He got up from the bed, slipped into his pants, and went over to the window. A policeman was standing outside. Paul opened the door. "Can I help you?"

The man flashed a badge. "Are you Paul Karppenin?"

"Yes."

"I'm Detective Neimi. I'd like to ask you a few questions about a missing girl."

Rachel jumped up from the bed. A missing girl? She quickly got dressed.

"Come in." Paul pointed to the kitchen. "We can talk there."

Rachel ran out from the bedroom. "What? Do you have news about Olivia?"

The detective looked confused. "Olivia? No, I'm here about Grace Mattson."

Rachel stepped back. "You're not here about my sister?"

"I'm here to talk to Mr. Karppenin about a missing girl." He looked at Rachel. "But I don't think it's the one you're interested in." The detective reached into his pocket, pulled out a small, transparent evidence bag, and set it down in front of Paul.

Paul stared at the gold necklace inside. "Where did you get this?"

"Do you recognize it?"

"It looks like the one I gave Grace for her birthday last year, but I don't know if it's the same." He looked at the detective. "Can I pick it up?"

The detective nodded.

Paul picked up the bag and stared at it. "It's a gold chain. I can't say it's the same one I gave Grace." He put it back on the table. "Where did you get it?"

Detective Neimi pulled out a small notebook and jotted something down. "This was found among the remains we discovered up near the Summit Peak Trail."

The color drained from Paul's face. "You mean, that body was...Grace?"

Rachel took a few steps back and stared at Paul.

"We're not a hundred percent sure. Our team's examining dental records now. I need to ask you a few questions."

Rachel suddenly felt ill. She went back to the bedroom and shut the door. How could this have happened? Her sister was missing, and she just slept with a guy whose girlfriend's body was found up on the mountain?

Rachel sat on the edge of the bed. She had to get out of there. A wave of nausea washed over her. She stumbled into the bathroom and vomited. After sitting on the toilet for a few minutes, she washed her face, rinsed out her mouth, and returned to the bedroom. She picked up her suitcase and started packing up her clothes.

Paul turned toward the bedroom. "Excuse me for a second."

He went in to Rachel. "Are you okay?"

She shook her head. "No, I sure as hell am not okay."

"What are you doing?"

"I gotta get out of here. I'm going back home."

Paul took her by the arm. "They still don't know who's up there. And whoever it is, I didn't have anything to do with it."

Tears ran down her face. "I don't know what to think. This…it's all just too much."

The detective called from the kitchen, "Mr. Karppenin, we can do this here or down at the station."

Paul pulled her closer. "Please. I know you're confused. Pack your things if that's what you want, but why don't you drive down to the bar. There's a nice diner across the street.

The Koffee Kup. Wait for me there. We can have breakfast. You need to eat something before you get on the road. Please."

Rachel grabbed her suitcase. "I don't know. Maybe."

Paul returned. "What do you want to ask me?"

"When was the last time you saw or spoke to Grace Mattson?"

He thought for a moment. "It was almost a year ago. Around September 22nd give or take a day or two."

Detective Neimi scribbled another note in his book. "And how do you know it was on that date?"

"My birthday's September 15th. Grace got drunk that night, and I'd had enough of her drinking. It took me about a week to work up the courage to tell her it was over."

"What happened then? How did she take it?"

"Not so good. She called me a bunch of names, accused me of cheating on her, and then packed up her stuff and left."

Detective Neimi leaned back and looked into the living room. "What happened then? Did you see her again?"

"No, she started going out with another guy for a few months, and the next thing I heard, she had packed up and moved to Chicago. I wasn't surprised. She'd been trying to get me to go there with her for almost a year."

The officer was scribbling madly when his pencil lead broke. He pulled out a blue pen and continued to make notes. "And you didn't want to move to Chicago with her?"

Paul smiled. "Hell no. I'd been there a few times. Saw the sights and everything, but no. I don't know how anybody could live there. You ever drive in that traffic?"

Detective Niemi ignored him. "How do you think that body ended up on a trail eighteen miles from your apartment?"

Paul tensed. "I have no idea. If it is Grace—and you said you don't know—she did like to hike up there." He stared at the detective. "I'm not very happy about how you phrased that question. It sounds like you think I had something to do with this. Well, just to be clear, I didn't."

"Calm down, Mr. Karppenin. I'm not suggesting anything. All I know is that a woman's body has been found near here, and somehow, based on the information you provided our office yesterday, you're involved with another girl who may have gone missing. Coincidences don't play a big part in police work, sir. If you didn't have anything to do with it, who do you think did?"

"First of all, I'm still trying to wrap my head around the idea that it could be Grace up there. It just doesn't seem possible. If it is, who would have done something like that?" He wished he had made a pot of coffee. "All I can tell you is that the guy she went out with after me had a bad reputation. You must know him, Vince Moretti."

The officer stopped writing. "Vincent Moretti? That's who she was going out with?"

Paul smiled. "Yeah, I thought you'd know him."

"Anybody else you can think of?"

"No, I really can't think of anyone who would want to hurt Grace."

Arnold poured himself another cup of coffee and sat back down at the kitchen table. He had forgotten to bring up his sling from the basement. He flexed his left arm. There was still some pain, but nothing like before. The redness had gone away. The peroxide must have done the trick.

He looked at the calendar on the side of the refrigerator. It was Friday. Damn. Why couldn't it be Tuesday? He needed to see Leslie again. That was the problem. How was he supposed to get all hot and bothered by that stranger downstairs? Oh, she was pretty, all right. But she wasn't Leslie.

He took a sip of coffee. Now with the whole house to himself, if he had Leslie downstairs, she'd probably be liking him by now. He stared at the empty chair across from him. Yep. She'd be sitting right there. Maybe she would have made him a nice breakfast. How long did it take for that Stockholm syndrome to kick in?

He finished his coffee and hurried down the stairs to his room in the basement. He sat behind his computer, typed in "Stockholm syndrome", and started reading.

Several minutes later, he pushed himself away from the screen. What? The FBI estimated only 8 percent of people actually exhibited it? 8 percent? That's all?

He slammed down the lid of his laptop. There was only an 8 percent chance that girl downstairs would grow to like him? 8 percent? That wasn't going to work. What was he going to do now? Something. He had to come up with something.

He went back to the kitchen and grabbed a Mountain Dew. A knock at the front door startled him. Who could that be? He'd notified all of the impending guests. Arnold snuck into the foyer, pressed himself against the wall, and peeked out the window. Shit! A cop! Arnold's chest tightened. Don't answer the door. Let him go away. No, they never go away. He'll just come back. Maybe with more cops.

Arnold slowly opened the door. "Good morning. How can I help you?"

"I'm Deputy Kevola. Can I come in?"

"Of course." He held the door open.

Deputy Kevola stepped into the foyer. "I'm looking into the possible disappearance of a woman named Olivia Thompson. I have reason to believe she stayed at your establishment recently." He glanced around the area. "Does that name sound familiar to you?"

"It certainly does, Deputy. She did stay here. She was with her boyfriend. I was getting ready to toss them out just before they decided to leave."

Arnold pulled open an antique desk drawer and rummaged through some manila folders. "Here's their paperwork. They stayed here Tuesday the eighteenth through Thursday the twentieth. They were supposed to check out on Friday, but they had a terrible fight Thursday night, and that's when they left. Good thing too. Like I said, they were about to get kicked out." Arnold paused. "You say she's missing?"

"Her sister filed a missing person's report yesterday. I was able to track down Ms. Thompson's boyfriend, Thomas Riggins. He told me they did have a fight, but he said Olivia decided not to leave with him. She didn't want anything to do with him. She told him she would find her own way home."

"Really! He said that? Well, that's ridiculous. Did he tell you how he was beating her? How he dragged her to the car and pushed her in?"

"He was hitting her?"

"Yes, I saw it with my own two eyes."

"And you didn't report this?"

Arnold blinked a few times. "Ah, well…I guess I should have. But to be frank, I was just glad they were leaving. All the time they were here, it was constant bickering. And then it got worse. Thank goodness we didn't have the other room rented. That would have been a disaster." He paused. "Oh, did her boyfriend mention that he owes us a hundred and twenty dollars for breaking a chair in their room along with an antique vase? No, I bet he didn't tell you about that, did he?"

The deputy shook his head. "No, he didn't say anything about that."

"I'm not surprised. Well, they stayed up in Room Two. Would you like to see it?"

"Sure."

The deputy followed him up the narrow staircase. Arnold opened a door and motioned for him to enter.

The deputy looked around for a few minutes and then walked over to a window. "Quite a view of the lake you got from up here."

"Yes, it's nice, isn't it? That's one of the reasons I get so many repeat customers."

The deputy turned. "I noticed you have a closed sign on the front door."

"Ah, yes. We're temporarily closed. We had a fire. The old barn behind the house burned down a few days ago. Smoke was everywhere. I had to air out the place. We also had supplies, you know, food and linens, stored there. I'm hoping to reopen sometime next week."

The deputy turned toward the door. "Can I get your name for my paperwork?"

"Spivey. Arnold Spivey."

"You mentioned *we* several times. Do you run this with someone else?"

Arnold stammered, "Ah, well…I did. My mother helped me. But she had a back operation a while ago, and it went bad. She's never left her wheelchair since."

Deputy Kevola jotted down a few notes. "Would I be able to speak to her?"

"You can. If you want to drive down to Grand Rapids. She's been staying with her sister for the last six weeks."

"So, she doesn't know anything about the missing girl, then. Right?"

Arnold shook his head. "Afraid not." Not wanting to answer any more questions, he ushered the deputy to the door and escorted him downstairs to the foyer.

Deputy Kevola pulled out a card and handed it to him. "If you think of anything else, give me a call."

Arnold took the card and set it on the desk. "I will."

They stepped out onto the porch. Arnold tried to keep a smile on his face as the deputy walked away. As the police cruiser disappeared down the road, Arnold turned to go back into the house. He stopped. A dark, reddish-brown stain was in the grass near the bottom step. He gripped the porch railing. It was blood. Mr. Jacobson's blood. How could that still be there after all the rain they had?

He went to the kitchen, filled a bucket with soapy water, and returned to the front yard. They'd be back. It was only a matter of time. How much time? Probably not a lot. He needed to come up with a solution to the problem in the coal bin.

Duck sat at the bar grinning. "Can you believe it, Paul? She pulled me into the library, shut the door, and we—"

"I know, I know. Dammit, Duck, you told me the story three times already. Good for you."

"Too bad about that Rachel chick. She just up and left. No goodbye or anything, right?"

Paul picked up the soda gun and filled a glass. "I was hoping to meet her at the diner, but when I finally got there, she wasn't around. I asked inside to see if she had come in and waited for me, but they told me nobody had been there that fit her description."

Duck frowned. "I should have never brought that newspaper in here. Seems like she freaked out when she saw that picture."

Paul nodded. "And having the detective knocking at my door this morning didn't help much either."

"He doesn't really think you had something to do with the missing girl, does he?"

Paul checked the bar to see if any customers needed his attention. "Yeah, I get the feeling he does."

"What are you going to do?" Duck asked.

"I need to start looking around. See if I can find out anything about Grace. What the hell happened? I've got to get that cop off my back. You know how people talk around here."

Rachel pulled her car over to the side of the road. This wasn't going to work. How could she go home and tell her mother that she had been up here for five days and had found out almost nothing. Her mother had been frantic the last few times they had spoken. She couldn't just run away. Maybe Paul was the key. Maybe he had something to do with both his old girlfriend and Olivia. After all, other than Tommy, wasn't he the last person to see her?

She made a U-turn and headed back to the mountains.

Chapter 16

FROM THE RUMBLINGS in her stomach, Olivia thought she must be on her second day without food or water.

She rolled over on the mattress. There it was again. That scraping noise from under the mattress. She reached under and pulled out the plastic spoon. She turned it over in her hand. There must be some way to use this. What about those awful prison shows that were on TV? Weren't they always sharpening things to use against each other? What did they call them? A shib? No, shiv. Yes, that was it. They called them shivs.

She knelt on the mattress and rubbed the handle against the rough concrete floor a few times. She ran her finger over the edge. It was sharper. She slipped off the mattress and started rubbing the spoon handle vigorously against the rough floor.

After fifteen minutes, she stopped and felt the tip. It was warm and sharp. She flexed the handle between her fingers. It was very pliable. One good stab and it would probably break into pieces. What could she use to reinforce it?

She looked around the room. Several small pieces of foam insulation were held in place near the door with wide

147

strips of masking tape. She peeled off a three inch section and wrapped it around the handle. Yes, that was better. She pulled off another piece and added it to the other tape.

There was a noise at the door. Olivia stuffed the spoon under the mattress and sat back against the wall just as the door swung open.

Arnold walked in holding a bag. He set it down on the end of the mattress. "Here's a few hamburgers." He stared at her for a moment. "What have you been up to?"

She tried to stay calm. "What do you mean?"

"You look guilty. Like a cat that ate the canary."

"The only thing I'm guilty of is wanting to go home."

He sat down on the chair. "Yeah. Nobody's ever happy. I'm stuck here in this house and want to get the hell out and see the world. You're away from home and want to go back. See? Nobody ever gets what they want."

She was about to say something, but stopped. What kind of convoluted logic was that? He could leave whenever he wanted to. Not her. "You're not wearing your sling. Is your arm getting better?"

He glanced down. "Yeah. I've been pouring peroxide on it every day. Guess it kicked in. It's still a little sore, but not like it used to be."

"I finished your book."

He sat back. "You did? Did you like it?"

"I did. I thought the author had quite an imagination. Do you have any other books I can read?"

Arnold rubbed his hands together. "Oh, yeah. I got a ton of them. That book you read is the first in a series. Do you want the next one or something different?"

"Why don't you get me something different, and then I'll read the next one."

"Okay. Sure. I'll go get it right now." Arnold sprang to his feet.

She looked over at the bag of food. A container of soda was sticking out of the top of the bag. "Oh, could I have some water? Like maybe a whole pitcher?"

"Um. A pitcher? I don't know about that, but I've got some bottled water upstairs I can get you."

Arnold left the room, but paused to bolt the door. He took the steps two at a time. This must be working. She was talking to him. She read the book, and she wanted to read more of his collection. She must be part of that 8 percent. He smiled. This may turn out to be better than he expected.

Olivia took a bite from one of the hamburgers. Kill him with kindness. She needed to gain his trust. Keep him off guard. Just when he wouldn't suspect anything, then she could strike.

She slipped her fingers under the mattress and felt the plastic spoon. It was still there. Her very own shiv. She finished the burger and reached for another one. Could she do it? Could she really do it? Stab him? Kill him? She shuddered. No, probably not.

Paul stared at the door of the Koffee Kup Kafe. Was she going to show? She hadn't been very nice to him after he and Grace had broken up. He glanced back down at the menu.

A flash of red hair caught his attention as Linda Phelps slid into the booth across from him. He said, "Hello. Thanks for coming."

Linda didn't respond for a moment and then said, "I really don't know what I'm doing here. I was very surprised to get your call. Why did you ask to meet me here?"

He wasn't surprised at the frosty reception. "Well, um, I … I wanted to talk about Grace."

"What about her?"

Paul sat back. "You've heard about the girl they found up on the Summit Peak Trail, haven't you?"

"Of course. How has that got anything to do with Grace?"

"Did you see the reconstruction they did? It was in the paper. Everyone thinks it looks like her."

Linda smiled. "That's crazy. I just talked to her…let me think. A month ago. No, maybe it was longer than that. Anyway, she was all depressed about moving back here. We had lunch." She paused. "Um, it didn't go very well."

Paul gave a start. "She moved back here? I thought she had a good job in Chicago."

Linda motioned for the waitress. "Can I get a cup of coffee, please?" She turned back to Paul. "They let her go. She got fired."

"What happened?"

"You know how she liked to drink? Well, I think Chicago was a little too much for her. She wanted to move there for so long, but once she finally made it, I think the city frightened her. I went to see her once, and wow, she was drinking pretty heavily."

Paul took a sip of coffee. "So she came back here?"

"Yeah. She tried moving back home, but that only lasted a few weeks. I told her it was a dumb idea. You remember how she didn't get along with her stepfather?"

Paul nodded. "Yeah. I heard some stories."

"Anyway, after that she got an apartment in Marquette, but she was only there about a month. She still wanted to live in a bigger city. The last I heard she was headed for Grand

Rapids." She took a sip of coffee. "I'm done with her. She tried to borrow money from me again. I told her no, and she went off on me."

"Yeah. She owes me some money too. I doubt I'll ever see it again." He smiled. "A good lesson learned."

"She wasn't getting along with her mother either. I guess they had a big fight when she was home. Grace said they hadn't talked since she left. The last time we got together, when she tried to borrow that money, she was really depressed. She didn't want to come back here. She felt bad because it didn't work out with you, and her time with Vince had been a nightmare. She was afraid of him."

Paul frowned. "Why was she afraid of him? I know he's a jerk, but afraid?"

"He pushed her around. Hit her a few times. He went crazy when she broke up with him. That's the main reason she moved to Chicago. To get away from him. Yeah, she was really depressed." Linda paused to sip her coffee.

"You should give her a call."

Linda grimaced. "I don't think so. I tried to call her after our disastrous lunch. She sounded drunk. It wasn't a great call. That drinking of hers has alienated her from just about everyone." She looked over at Paul. "But I don't need to tell you that, do I. Let's just say she isn't a friendly drunk."

"No. That's for sure."

"Oh, I heard about Russo's closing. I can't believe it. It's been here for as long as anyone can remember."

"Yeah. I'm looking around for another job, but you know this area. I may have to move. All thanks to Grace's stepdad."

"Mr. Mattson? What's he got to do with it?"

151

"He owns the building. He made the decision to tear it down."

Her eyes got wide. "Are you kidding? What a shame." She looked over at the clock. "Oh, I've got to go."

She slid out of the booth and hesitated. "Paul, it's too bad you guys had to break up. You were really good for Grace. You kept her in line and treated her with respect."

Paul smiled. "Tell that to the detective who's asking me a thousand questions."

When Rachel stepped into the office of the White Pine Motel, the desk clerk waved hello. "You're back. I can put you in the same room if you'd like. We just got it ready."

She hesitated and then walked up to the desk. This wasn't going to be easy. She had practiced her speech about a hundred times. "Um, hello, Walter. Yes, well...I have a slight problem."

"What is it?"

"Ah, this is just stupid. But anyway, I'm almost out of money. I'm up here looking for my sister. I could pay for one more night, but then...I was wondering, do you have some things I could do, some job, or something? Maybe I could work off the room for another few days. I know it sounds stupid, but I just thought that maybe it might work."

Walter thought for a moment. "Give me a minute." He stepped into a small alcove that was next to the office and closed the door. He returned a few minutes later with a big smile on his face. "Okay. That was easy."

Rachel stood waiting for him to continue.

"I just called my uncle. He owns this place. I told him about your situation, and how I had just about scared you to death the other day. He said as long as we're not filled up, you can stay here at no charge." He handed her a key.

"Are you sure? I'll be happy to work. There must be something I can do? I can pay for tonight."

Walter shook his head. "No, you've got enough on your plate."

Rachel ran around the desk and gave him a big hug. "Thank you! Thank you so much!"

Walter looked embarrassed. He hesitated and then said, "Did you know we got another person missing around here?"

"What? You do? Who is it?"

"A guy named Frank Jacobson."

"When did this happen?"

"I saw it on the news a few days ago. His truck's missing too. He was separated from his wife. She thinks he's missing, but some of his buddies say he just took off. I don't know. Something's going on here this summer. It's just not natural."

Rachel thought about what he said. "Do me a favor, will you?"

"What's that?"

"If you hear anything more about the missing man, let me know."

"I'll do that."

"Thank you."

She went back to the car, grabbed her bag, and returned to her old room. She put a few of her things away and then picked up the motel phone. "Hello, Elaine. It's Rachel. Is Mom there?"

Elaine took a deep breath. "Your mother's taken a turn for the worse. I called social services, and we've got a nurse here now. It...it was more than I could handle. I'm sorry, but—."

Rachel gripped the receiver. "How bad is she? Should I come home? I...damn....I just got my room comped. I'd like to stay a few days longer, but maybe—"

"No, Rachel. Stay. It's nothing that urgent. It was just that your mother was having difficulty breathing. They've got her on oxygen now, and she does look a little better."

Rachel put her head in her hands and tried to think. "Elaine, what should I do? Should I come home?"

There was a pause. "I don't know. If you come home without having any information about your sister, I think that would be even harder on your mother. Why don't you stay a few more days? Give me your number at the motel. I'll call you if she takes a turn for the worse."

Chapter 17

DUCK HEARD SOMEONE walk up behind him as he sat working at his desk. He turned. Dieter stood there with his arms folded. He had a sour look on his face.

"I'm sorry I was late today, Dieter. Something important came up, and I had to talk to one of my friends. But don't worry, I can stay late and make up the time."

"No need to stay late, Mr. Lindquist." Dieter pointed to the desk. "You need to pack up your tools. You're finished."

"Finished? No, I'm hardly finished. Remember, you said it was going to take a few more days to get everything—"

"It doesn't matter what I said. Your work here is done."

Duck pulled off his eye loop and stood up. "I know what this is about. Look, I don't think it's anybody's business what I do after hours. If I want to have a drink with—"

Dieter interrupted. "A ring is missing."

"What?"

"Mrs. Haverhill has informed me that a ring you were supposed to work on last week has gone missing."

"Which one?"

"The twenty-eight carat, green diamond ring."

"I remember it." Duck wiped sweat from his forehead. "How couldn't I? I cleaned it and put it back in the strong box with all the other pieces I worked on that day. How could it be missing?"

"That's what Mrs. Haverhill would like to know. That ring was once owned by the Archduke of Austria in 1848. It's a priceless piece of history, sir. You must remember what you did with it."

"I just told you. I cleaned it like all the other jewelry and returned it to the strongbox."

Dieter stepped forward and started putting the jewelry that was scattered about the table into another metal box. "I'm afraid your employment here is terminated, and I will be notifying the authorities of your transgression."

"You got to be kidding me. You think I stole that ring?"

"Please, sir. Let's not cause a scene. Pack up your things. I'll escort you to the door."

Duck gathered his tools and followed Dieter into the dining room. "I know what you're up to. You found out about my date with Juliette, and you've drummed up some ridiculous story or hidden the ring yourself so that I'd be forced to leave."

Dieter held the large wooden door open. "Good day, sir."

Duck stood outside the chateaux in bewilderment as the door slammed shut behind him.

Arnold straightened the cushions on the sofa. He glanced around the room. Everything looked in order. Tonight was the night he was going to let Olivia come upstairs and watch TV.

The day before had been wonderful. When he had returned with the water, Olivia had carried on a conversation with him for over an hour. She had laughed at his jokes and had seemed genuinely interested in hearing about him. There really was something to that Stockholm syndrome.

He entered the kitchen and pulled open the refrigerator. The red wine was cool. Was red wine supposed to be chilled? Must be. Who'd want to drink warm wine?

He held up two glasses to the light. Smudges. Those needed to go. He polished the glasses with a towel until they looked perfect. Time to get her.

The door to the coal bin swung open. Olivia turned. Something was different. Why was he all dressed up?

Arnold swayed from one foot to the other. "I was wondering if you'd like to come upstairs and have a shower. Maybe watch some TV with me."

"Go upstairs?"

"Yeah. I thought that you'd probably like a shower by now, and we could maybe watch a little TV."

"Really?" She moved her hand down the side of the mattress. Should she take the shiv with her? She slid her fingers under the fabric.

"What are you doing?"

She shoved the spoon away from the edge and stood up. "I'm coming with you." She stepped closer. "Thank you."

He pointed to her suitcase. "Get some new clothes. I'm sure you're sick of what you've been wearing."

She pulled out a different outfit and some clean underwear. She grabbed a toothbrush.

As they ascended the stairs, Arnold said, "I don't want to have to say this, but don't try anything. I'm doing you a big favor here, and I don't want you to ruin it."

She stepped into the kitchen. "I won't." Immediately the image of Arnold's mother flashed across her mind. She shuddered.

He showed her where the downstairs bathroom was and where he had set out a towel and washcloth.

Olivia hesitated. Her hair was greasy, but she was afraid to take her clothes off and get into that shower. She tried the lock on the door. It worked. Too bad there wasn't a window she could crawl out of.

She spent half an hour under the warm water. It felt wonderful. She dried herself and put on her fresh clothes.

When she stepped out of the bathroom, Arnold pulled the red wine bottle out of the refrigerator, poured two glasses, and handed one to her. "Here."

"Wine? Well, this is a surprise." She followed him into the living room and took a seat at the edge of the couch where he had motioned for her to sit.

He picked a well-worn chair. "There's a movie coming on in a few minutes. It's a comedy. I thought that would be the best one for us to watch."

"Okay."

After the first ten minutes, Arnold had finished his wine. He stood up. "Would you like more?"

She held up her glass. It was still three-quarters full. "No, I'm fine." A large gray cat jumped onto the couch and snuggled next to her.

As he returned to the kitchen for a refill, she glanced over at the foyer and the front door. It was only about twenty feet away. One quick sprint and she could be down those front steps. Was it locked? Did he have it rigged some way so it wouldn't open?

He sat back down. "I see Daisy likes you."

She glanced down at the cat. "How old is she?"

Arnold thought for a second. "About nine. Um, do you like the movie?"

She nodded. "Yes, it's very funny."

An hour later, Arnold had finished three more glasses of wine. When he returned with the fourth, he didn't sit in the chair. He took a seat on the opposite end of the couch. As he sat down, some wine spilled onto his pants. "Oh, shit. I've got to get this out. These are my good pants." He ran to the bathroom.

Olivia took a sip of wine and continued to watch the movie. She looked over at the front door. Now's the time. It would only take two seconds to make it to the door. She stood up.

"Where you going?" He was behind her.

She let out a little squeak. "You scared me."

"Where were you going?"

She pointed to her glass. "I thought I'd get a refill. Is that okay?"

"Yeah. Go ahead."

When she returned, Arnold was sitting near her place on the couch. He was in his underwear. His pants were neatly folded on the sofa next to him.

She stopped. "What are you doing?"

He smiled. "You know. Let's have some fun."

She stepped back toward the kitchen.

Arnold sprang from the couch and took her by the arm. "What's the matter? I thought things were going good?"

She tried to pull away. "Watching TV and having sex are two different matters."

"Fine. If that's what you want, then it's back to the basement with you." He pushed her toward the steps and

159

quickly walked back to the living room and pulled his pants back on.

As he led her down the stairs, Olivia looked for something she could grab to use as a weapon. When they approached the door to the coal bin, Olivia noticed the two-by-four screwed to the outside and the iron latches. "What's that?"

"Reinforcement. The only way you'll ever get out of here is when I let you out. And that won't be happening anytime soon unless that attitude of yours changes." He pushed her inside, slid the dead bolt shut, and slammed the two-by-four securely into the metal latch.

Rachel sat at the bar in Sudsy's and drank her beer. At first, because of her money situation, she had hesitated even going out at all. She'd have to buy the first drink, but after that, it wouldn't be a problem to score free drinks. She'd spent enough time in bars to have figured that out.

The guy next to her was a salesman, Norm Swenson. He sold logging equipment in Michigan, Wisconsin, and Minnesota. "How about another one," Norm asked, pushing his fat face a little too close.

"Okay, why not." She tipped her bottle to make sure nothing was left for the bartender to take away. As she put the empty bottle on the bar, she noticed Paul walking toward her. This was going to be interesting.

He slid onto the stool next to her. "This is a surprise. I thought you were going home?"

"I was. I got almost halfway back and then changed my mind. I couldn't go home with nothing to tell Mother. Our neighbor's watching her. She's not doing well. If I showed up without any information, I don't know what would happen."

Norm tapped her on the shoulder. "Hey. Who's that guy? I thought you were talking to me?"

"I'm sorry. This is Paul. He's...a friend of mine." She turned back to Paul. "And this is Norm. He sells logging equipment."

Paul reached across Rachel and shook Norm's hand. "Hi. Nice to meet you. Don't let me interrupt." He whispered in Rachel's ear, "I've got some news about Grace. If you get a minute, I'd like to tell you about it." He pointed across the room. "I'm going to go say hello to Charlie. Come see me when you can."

Rachel talked with the salesman for another twenty minutes and then went over to where Paul and Charlie were standing.

Charlie smiled. "Hello."

Paul stepped closer. "Charlie's going to California tomorrow."

"That's nice," Rachel replied. "Business or pleasure?"

"Pleasure. I'm visiting my sister. She's just had her second kid. I'm going to play uncle for a few days."

Paul turned to her. "Have you ever been there?"

"No, but I'd like to someday."

Paul motioned toward a booth. "If you don't mind, Rachel and I have a few things we need to catch up on."

Charlie glanced up at the bar clock. "That's fine. I've got to get home and start packing."

"You haven't started packing yet?" Rachel asked.

Charlie smiled. "Not yet." He put some money on the bar. "I'll see you guys when I get back."

After he left, Rachel followed Paul over to the booth. "I had a long talk with one of Grace's best friends yesterday. She told me Grace moved back here from Chicago a few months ago."

Rachel tensed. "So it could be her up there?"

"Nobody knows. I tried to get Linda to call her and see if she answered. She wouldn't do it. She said Grace was drunk the last time she talked to her. The conversation didn't go well, so she wouldn't make the call."

"Why don't *you* call her?" Rachel asked.

"I tried, but she must have changed her number."

"Where did she move to? Somewhere around here?"

"Marquette. It's about a hundred miles east of us. Her friend said she had lost her job in Chicago, and she was depressed because she had to move back here."

"Why did she come back?"

"Linda thought Chicago turned out to be a little too much for her. Then when she lost her job, she probably returned to get back on her feet."

"And then she didn't like it once she got back?" Rachel asked.

"Grace didn't want to come back because she wasn't happy about our breakup, and she was afraid of that guy she went out with after me." Paul paused. "I don't blame her. He's a real piece of work."

Rachel asked, "What do you mean?"

"I guess Vince pushed her around a little, which I don't doubt. He's got that kind of reputation. For the life of me, I can't understand why she was going out with him."

Rachel nodded. "Yeah. I ask myself the same question about my sister."

Chapter 18

THE NEWS HAD just reported that, with the rain they were expecting, it would be the second wettest July on record. Paul switched off the television. He didn't have to be at work until two o'clock, and with this weather they could probably get by without him even longer.

His meeting the day before with Grace's friend Linda had just created more questions in his mind. He went over to the kitchen window. What a miserable day. Windy and rainy. Maybe he should pay a visit to Grace's mother. See what she had to say.

Paul threw a rain breaker over his flannel shirt and headed out the door.

The road up to the Mattson's place was wet and muddy. The house sat behind a long split rail fence. A horse barn was to the left. Nothing had changed since Paul's last visit. That was the day he and Grace had ridden horses most of the afternoon. Grace loved to ride. The property consisted of forty acres. There were six horses, no neighbors, and plenty of riding trails. A red Toyota RAV was parked in front of a four-car garage.

Paul pulled the hood of his rain gear over his head and ran up to the front door. He knocked. The steady downpour made a racket on the tin roof. He knocked again.

The door swung open. Mrs. Mattson waved him inside. Paul didn't recognize her at first. It looked as if she had gone without sleep for several days.

"I was wondering if you'd be coming by," she said.

"I wanted to see you and find out about Grace. I don't know if you've seen the paper, but—"

"Oh, I've seen it." Mrs. Mattson slowly collapsed on a couch and covered her face with her hands. "It's her. My baby Gracie." She pulled a crumpled tissue out of her pocket and wiped her eyes. "I got a visit early this morning. Dental records confirmed it was her."

Paul reached over and took her hand. "Oh, I'm so sorry." Such terrible news. He looked around. Why was she alone? "Where's Mr. Mattson?"

She stuffed the tissue back into her pocket. "He's gone. We…we recently separated." She fought back tears. "He's renting a place in Houghton. He doesn't want anyone to know about it, though. He's running for a state representative seat." She pulled the tissue out again and dabbed her eyes. "You know. Wouldn't look good."

Paul sat in stunned silence. "I…I don't know what to say. I'm so sorry. About everything."

She looked over at him with red, teary eyes. "It's nice to see you, Paul. I wish you two had never broken up. I don't think this would have ever happened if the two of you were still together. You were good for Grace."

Her statement stabbed him like a knife. "Um, what happened, Mrs. Mattson? Did the authorities say?"

She shook her head. "Not yet. I don't think they know." She quickly added, "Gracie moved back here. Did you know?"

"I only learned about it yesterday."

"Gracie wasn't happy about having to come back here. But when she lost her job, she didn't know what to do. I warned her about her drinking." She looked up at Paul. "You know what I'm talking about."

"Yes. It could be an issue."

She stood up. "I just made some fresh coffee. Can I get you some?"

Paul nodded. "Yes, please."

She left the room and returned with two cups. She handed one to Paul. "So what brings you here?"

"I was hoping to hear that Grace was just fine and still in Chicago. The police have been asking me questions like they think I had something to do with this."

Mrs. Mattson reached over and squeezed his hand. "That's ridiculous. You and Grace were good together. Better than that damn Vince." She wiped her eyes. "It's been a rough few months. Fred moved out shortly after Grace came back from Chicago."

"She stayed here?"

"Only for a week or so. Then she got a place in Marquette. She wasn't happy there either. She was bound and determined to live in a bigger city. Fred gave her money to help her get settled in Grand Rapids."

Paul sipped his coffee. That's what Linda had said.

After a long, uncomfortable pause, Mrs. Mattson said, "I don't know how much Gracie told you about Fred, but they didn't get along very well."

"I've heard some rumors to that effect."

"A few years after my first husband, Gracie's father, died, I met Fred. We got married. It happened fast. Probably too fast." She looked over at Paul and lowered her voice. "You don't really know a person like you should."

Paul nodded.

"Anyway, everything was fine with Gracie. Oh, it was rough at the beginning. She missed her dad, and she didn't want to let Fred take his place. Things started to get better for a few years until she started sneaking out, drinking, carrying on and such. She settled down a bit when she met you."

Mrs. Mattson's hand began to shake. She set her cup down on the coffee table. "Fred really lost it when Gracie started going out with that Vince guy. And then he found out about Vince hitting her. It took everything I had to talk him out of going down there and beating Vince up. Can you imagine what that would have done to the business if he had gone and done such a foolish thing like that?" She tried to fight back tears. "And now she's gone."

Paul looked around. "Are you all alone here? Do you have someone who can come over and be with you?"

"My sister's coming in from Iowa. I expect her anytime. In fact, I thought it was her when I heard your car drive up."

"That's good." He stood up. "I don't want to bother you. If there's anything I can do, please give me a call. I'm still working down at the bar. You can always reach me there." Paul paused. "Well, for the next two months, anyway."

"I'm sorry about Fred wanting to tear down that beautiful old building. I pleaded with him to pick another location for that car wash. But he wouldn't listen. Said that corner would be a gold mine. I tried. Believe me, I tried." She stood up and gave him a hug. "Thank you for coming."

Paul slowly walked to his car. It had stopped raining. How sad. Her daughter was dead and the poor woman didn't even have her husband around to comfort her.

As Paul headed back down the narrow driveway, he had to pull over to let another car go by. An older woman was driving. That must have been Mrs. Mattson's sister. Thank goodness she had someone to stay with her.

Arnold fed the cat and pushed open the kitchen window. Finally some sunshine. It would be nice to air out the house. He wished it was Tuesday. It had been almost two weeks since he had last seen Leslie and her girlfriend at lunch. Since nobody had stopped by the house and asked him anything about her break-in, he was confident that tomorrow it would be safe enough to drive into town and watch them have lunch at the Koffee Kup. Hell, maybe he'd join them. Well, not really join them, but maybe take a table on the other side of the restaurant. His arm didn't have to be in that damn sling anymore. He would still have to wear a long sleeve shirt to hide the bite marks, but with this weather, he'd probably be wearing a jacket over his shirt anyway.

That left the girl. Something had to be done with her. Couldn't have both of them downstairs. He already had the rat poison and the hamburger for that Doberman. He'd have to wait a few days after the dog died to try to get Leslie again. Let things settle down for a while. Maybe a week. A week? That was a long time.

But the girl. Just let her stay down there for a few more days? How long could she go without food or water? No, that would be torture. It would take too long. Something quick. He thought of how Mr. Jacobson had crumpled by the front porch. Yeah. It had to be quick.

Rachel sat in the diner and watched as the gray clouds were replaced with patches of blue sky. She was bundled up in a blouse and jacket and was still cold. The cool dampness of the air seemed to penetrate every layer.

She stared down at the menu but couldn't think of food. Here she was, on borrowed time and completely out of ideas. Should she call Paul? He had taken her to some different places. Maybe he could point her in a new direction. Could he be trusted, or would she end up missing too?

She reached in her purse for her cellphone and paused. What about his old girlfriend? The police had wanted to talk to him. Why? The boyfriend's always a suspect. But he wasn't her boyfriend. At least not at the time. But they still wanted to ask him questions.

She took a sip of her coffee. Sitting there with no ideas wasn't going to get her anywhere. She pulled out her phone and called his number.

She felt better after talking with him. He was ten minutes away, and he wanted to join her for lunch. She dialed her mother's number. "Mom. Hello, it's Rachel."

"How are you, honey? Have you found out anything?"

Rachel pushed the phone tighter to her ear. "Can you speak up a little?"

"What have you found out?"

"Ah, well, a few things, Mom. I don't want to get into everything now. It's a little complicated. The police are helping. That's a good thing."

"When are you coming home?"

"I'd say in a few days. Two or three more days. How are you feeling?"

"Better. I'm feeling better. I got a nurse now."

"You sound tired, Mother."

"Yes, I'm kind of tired. Maybe you could call back?"

"Sure. I'll call back." She ended the call and leaned back in the booth. That didn't even sound like her mother. Her voice was so weak. There was no urgency in her tone. Maybe she should call back? Really? She grabbed a napkin and fought back tears. She didn't want Paul to see her like this.

A few minutes later he slid into the booth across from her. "I'm so glad you called."

"I was surprised you weren't at work."

He glanced at the silver and red diner clock. "I should be there in forty-five minutes."

The waitress came by. He ordered coffee. "I've had a very depressing morning."

Rachel raised her eyebrows. "Really?"

"I went and visited Grace's mother."

Rachel sat silent for a moment. "Oh, how did that go?"

"Not so good. This morning they told her that the body up on the mountain was definitely Grace."

Rachel's mouth fell open. "Oh, no!"

"Have you heard anything on TV?"

She shook her head.

"I'm surprised word hasn't gotten out yet. I guess they want to give Mrs. Mattson enough time to notify the rest of her family."

Rachel looked up. "What happened?"

"They don't know. At least they're not saying anything to her mother."

The waitress came over with Paul's coffee, and they ordered lunch.

Rachel picked up a creamer. "I wonder how Grace ended up on that mountain."

169

"Both her girlfriend and her mother indicated that she was depressed. She didn't want to leave Chicago. Coming back home was some sort of defeat for her. She had gone to the big city, and it hadn't worked out. Her dreams were dashed."

"She killed herself?"

Paul grimaced. "There's a giant step from being depressed to suicide. Grace had spunk. I just can't see her giving up. I could see her sticking around here long enough to save enough money to move somewhere else. And she was. She was going to move someplace not as big as Chicago, but a lot bigger than here."

"Okay. If she didn't kill herself, what happened?"

"I'm hearing more nasty things about the guy she went out with after me. He was hitting her. Grace's stepdad found out and went crazy. He wanted to go over and beat him up. Mrs. Mattson talked him out of it."

Rachel raised an eyebrow. "Probably a good idea." She sighed. "I talked to my mom just now. She sounded terrible. Very weak. I don't know how much longer I can stay here. I'm thinking a few more days at the most."

Chapter 19

ARNOLD WAITED UNTIL midnight. For the last two hours, he had gone back and forth about what would be the best way to get this done. Gun? No, the deer rifle he had used on Mr. Jacobson was too big to try to sneak into the coal bin with any element of surprise.

Knife? Too up front and personal. Yes, it had worked on his mother, but that was different. He had only grabbed it in the middle of his rage. He didn't have any rage for the girl downstairs. Hell, he hardly knew her.

Finally he decided on something simple. No mess. A plastic bag. He could pull it over her head from behind. Hold it tight, and everything would be over in a matter of minutes. He knew exactly where he could get one.

He stepped into his mother's bedroom, opened the closet door, and slipped off a large dry cleaning bag from one of her Sunday dresses. That should do it.

He balled it up and stuffed it into his pocket.

Olivia was sleeping when the lights came on. She shielded her eyes from the brightness. What time was it?

Arnold stood in the doorway. "Stand up and turn around."

She grabbed the blanket and pulled it close. "I'm not putting on that teddy."

"I said stand up."

Still sitting on the mattress, she inched back closer to the wall.

He sprang toward her and grabbed for her arm.

She pulled away.

Arnold screamed, "Get up!"

She kicked at him through the blanket, and he stumbled backwards. She jumped to her feet and held the blanket out in front of her. As he got to his knees, she threw it over him and sprang for the door.

Arnold struggled out from under the covering and reached for her ankle. He grabbed hold of her leg, dragged her back inside, and slammed the door shut. He glared at her. "Enough of your shit." As Olivia struggled to free herself, he pulled out the bag.

Behind him, from the other side of the door, there was a scraping sound followed by a dull thud. Arnold stopped. "No!" He spun around and pushed on the door. It didn't move. He turned and glared at Olivia. His eyes were bulging. "Damn you! You...you've locked us in!"

Olivia jumped onto the mattress and felt under it for the plastic spoon. Where was it? Her fingers reached along the cement floor. There! As she grabbed it, Arnold was on her again. She struggled as he forced the plastic bag over her head.

His hands were holding the bag over her face. Every time she tried to breathe, the bag was sucked into her mouth. As she jabbed the spoon toward him, he took his hand from her throat and grabbed for her arm. She felt the spoon connect to something.

His grip loosened from her throat.

She stepped back, pulled the bag from her head, and sucked in a deep breath of cool air.

Arnold was holding his face. Blood was oozing from a thin red line that ran from the corner of his right eye down to his cheekbone. He reached over and slapped her across the face with his bloody hand. "I should have killed you the minute I brought you down here!"

She lunged at him with the spoon.

He stepped to the side and then threw himself toward her. She slashed at his neck with the sharpened handle of the spoon. It ripped across the back of his knuckles and snapped into two pieces.

He stared down at his hand. "What the—?"

Olivia kicked him hard in the groin. As he bent over, she tried to knee him in the face. She lost her balance and tumbled to the hard concrete floor. He rolled on top of her and reached for her throat again.

As she struggled to get out from under him, Olivia jabbed what was left of the spoon up at him. The pressure on her neck let up. She pushed him off and jumped to her feet.

Arnold struggled to stand. He swayed for a few seconds and then pulled the broken spoon handle out of his neck. A stream of warm blood squirted out and hit Olivia.

He pushed his hand against the deep opening in his neck and fell to his knees. More blood gushed between his fingers. He fell to his side. After a few minutes, he stopped moving. The mattress was soaked with blood.

Olivia ran over to the door and pushed against it. It didn't budge. Somehow it had locked itself when he pulled her inside. She pounded on the door with her fists and called out.

There was no response. She looked back over toward Arnold. He hadn't moved.

Chapter 20

RACHEL ROLLED OVER in bed and opened her eyes. Where was Paul? She smelled coffee. He must be making breakfast. Bacon too. She snuggled back under the blankets and thought about the night before. What time had they gone to bed? It didn't matter. It had been a wonderful night.

She slipped on her bra and panties and tiptoed into the kitchen. "You got any coffee for the girl you ravaged last night?"

He jumped. "Jeez, don't sneak up on me when I'm in the middle of turning hot bacon. And furthermore, I think it was you who did the ravaging."

She nestled against him. "I'll take the blame."

The breakfast hit the spot. Rachel poured a second cup of coffee. "What's on your agenda today?"

Paul glanced at the clock. "I'm going to work later this afternoon, but I thought I'd try to find good old Vince and ask him a few questions."

"You're lucky. You have ideas and things you want to check out. I don't know why I'm still here. I guess it's because I can't bear the thought of going home and telling my mother I haven't found out anything about Olivia."

"I'd take you with me, but I don't know where I'm going to find him. He used to hang out over at the Fox's Den. It's a nasty place. I wouldn't want you anywhere near there." He set his plate in the sink. "Why don't you go down to the police station and see what they've done, if anything."

"That's a good idea. You made breakfast. I'll clean up the kitchen."

"Oh, I talked to Charlie yesterday. He said to say hello."

"How was his trip?"

"He had to find a place to stay. His sister's house is only 850 square feet."

Rachel dried a cup. "Really? That's small. I heard things are really expensive out there."

"I know. Charlie had a fit about how much hotels cost. He found a place some guy was renting out near his sister. It's one of those airbnb Internet deals. He said it was a lot cheaper than a regular motel."

Rachel turned. "Wait a minute. An airbnb. Maybe that's where Olivia and Tommy stayed. Do they have those here?"

"I don't know. Let's get on the computer and find out."

Rachel followed him to a desk in the living room.

After a few minutes on the computer, Paul pointed to a pad of paper and a pencil. "Write this down. I found two places. One's right in town on Superior Street. Here's the number." He read her the phone number and gave her the address. "And there's another one about ten miles out of town near the entrance to the state park. It's at 156 Turner Lane."

Rachel looked up from the notepad. "I can't believe I never thought of this. I'll check them out right after I go to the police station."

"Well, what have we here? You out slummin' or something?" the bartender asked as Paul walked into the Foxy Den.

He took a seat at the bar. "Hey, Gus. It's been a while. How've you been?"

Gus held up his left hand. "Chopped off two fingers a few months ago, but other than that, it's all good."

Paul leaned closer. "Damn. How'd you do that?"

"I was doing some chainsaw work out at the cabin. I'd had a few beers. Probably not a good idea. Anyway, the blade got stuck in a pine tree and kicked back. Lucky it didn't take off my whole hand. Anyway, what brings you in here today? You ain't working?"

"Yeah. Later this afternoon. I'm looking for Vince. He still hangs around here, doesn't he?"

Gus's smile disappeared. "He does, unfortunately. I don't suppose you're over here recruiting him as a customer for Russo's. You want a drink?"

Paul laughed. "Hardly. I wanted to ask him a few questions about Grace. Give me a Coke."

"Grace Mattson?"

"Yeah."

"Hey, that reminds me. Have you seen that face reconstruction of the girl they found up on the mountain?"

Paul nodded. "Yeah, I know. It looks a lot like Grace." He stopped. It wasn't his business to be giving out information the authorities hadn't revealed yet.

"That's what I thought. Is that why you're looking for Vince? Something to do with Grace?"

"That's part of it," Paul replied.

"He normally comes in here on Wednesday nights. Plays darts with a rowdy crowd. The Hubbard brothers and a few of their friends."

Paul nodded. "That sounds like it would be his bunch."

"You're still friends with Duck Lindquist, aren't you?"

"I sure am. He came into the bar with a real pretty French girl the other night."

"Did you know he got canned from his job over at the Haverhill mansion?"

"What? He was all excited about that deal. What happened?"

"They caught him stealing. Kicked him off the property."

Paul stared at Gus. "Who told you that? I have a very hard time believing Duck's a thief."

Gus poured himself a shot of whiskey. "His brother. Barney comes in here all the time."

"And you believe him? They've been on the outs for years." Paul shook his head. "Small towns. Everybody knows everybody else's business. I still don't believe Duck stole anything. You should have seen how excited he was about getting that job." He stood up and slapped a ten dollar bill on the bar. "I'll be back tomorrow night. Do me a favor. Don't mention I was here to Vince."

Gus downed the shot. "No problem. Hey, I hear Russo's is closing in a few months."

"Looks that way. Grace's step-dad's tearing the building down."

"If you need a job, come and see me. Maybe we could get some of your customers to come over here."

Paul smiled. "Thanks, Gus. I'll keep that in mind."

A county deputy stepped into a small conference room. He was holding a manila folder. "Put that out. You can't be smoking in here."

Rachel stubbed out her cigarette on the bottom of her shoe. "I had to have something to do when you stuck me in this claustrophobia-inducing room for twenty minutes."

The man coughed and waved his hand. "The chief's not going to be happy about this." He sat down across from her and pulled out some papers. "I don't know if you remember me, but I'm Deputy Kevola. I was assigned your case after we talked."

"I remember. Have you done anything? I thought I would have heard from you by now."

"I've looked into a few things. I was going to update you today or tomorrow. Problem is, I don't have very much to tell you."

"What *can* you tell me?"

"I called Thomas Riggins' number as you suggested. His mother answered. She said she would have him call me, and he did. Called me back the next day."

"Really? That's interesting. When I talked to her, she said she had no way of contacting him."

"He's staying with a friend in New York City. He just got a job detailing cars."

Rachel's eyes narrowed. "I thought he was going to college. That's what Olivia told my mother."

"He said his grades weren't good, and he lost his scholarship. I'll check into that. Anyway, about your sister. He claims they got into a big fight. She told him she didn't want anything to do with him, and that she'd find a way home by herself. He gave me the address of the place where they stayed. It's way out on Turner Lane."

Rachel gave a start. "Turner Lane? I can't believe it. I've checked every motel around here. I never even thought about people who rent out their places on the Internet. We just came up with that idea a few hours ago. Turner Lane was one of the places I was going to check out after I left here."

Deputy Kevola glanced down at his notes again. "A young man runs it. Arnold Spivey. I went out there and talked to him. He rents out rooms in his house. He confirmed the fact that your sister and her boyfriend had a fight. But he said Mr. Riggins forced your sister into the car the night they left, and they just drove off. He said he was glad to see them go. They'd been fighting the whole time they were there and had upset some guests. He was about to ask them to leave."

Rachel took a deep breath. "Tommy! What did she see in that creep?"

The deputy nodded. "He has a bad record with women. I'm setting up a meeting with the 79th precinct in New York City. I want them to administer a lie detector test on him."

"Would he do it?"

"Surprisingly, it was his idea."

Rachel sat back in her chair and tried to process everything the deputy had said. "I'm sorry for my attitude when I came in this morning. I…I just assumed you hadn't taken my report seriously. Thank you for everything you've done. But where's Olivia?"

Deputy Kevola closed his folder. "That's the question, isn't it."

Chapter 21

PAUL HAD BEEN BACK working at Russo's for a few hours when Duck came in. He took a seat at the bar where Paul was washing glasses. "You're never going to believe what happened over at the Haverhill place."

Paul put his index finger to his temple. "Ah, let me think. You got caught having sex with the hot French girl…no, that's probably not it. Um, you met old Mrs. Haverhill, and she's fallen madly in love with you and wants to steal you away to a sea-side resort in Monaco. Hmmm. No, that's probably not it. Oh, I know. Speaking of stealing, you pocketed a few rare gems from the estate, got caught, and now you're going to prison for the rest of your life. Yeah. That's probably what happened."

"Very funny. How did you hear about that? I only mentioned it to two people, and I told them to keep their traps shut about it."

Paul smiled. "Duck, we live in a town of a thousand people. Everybody knows everybody's business. Those two people you told, each told two more, who each told two more. Actually, I was in the Foxy Den and heard it from Gus, the bartender."

"What? Gus? How the hell did he find out?"
"From your brother."

"Barney? I haven't talked to him in six months."

"Like I said. Welcome to a small town. Now what happened? I know you didn't steal anything. You were very excited about that job."

"No shit. Can I get a beer? You'd think they'd hire some decent help around here."

"Okay, okay. Hold your horses." Paul poured him a draft.

"Yeah, I did like that job. They paid me well, fed me great lunches, and I got to meet Juliette." Duck took a sip of beer. "That was the problem. That damn German guy had his eye on her, and he got pissed off when she started showing me some attention. I know that's what happened."

"I can see being jealous, but accusing a man of theft. Now that's a little harsh."

Duck nodded. "You're right. I mean, I haven't heard from the cops or anything, but what if they file some kind of report. Hell, even now my name seems to be mud all over town. Even my brother's spreading rumors about me. If the store over in Marquette hears about this, they'll can me too."

"You don't want to lose your reputation. You need to fight back."

Duck shrugged. "How do I do that?" He let out a big sigh and motioned for Paul to come closer.

Paul asked, "What?"

"I've been thinking about something, but I need some advice."

"Okay."

Duck leaned over the bar and lowered his voice. "Something strange is going on around here. We've got a woman's skull they found up on the mountain and a missing girl, Rachel's sister. That's two women. Now, shit like that never happens here."

Paul looked at him. "Yeah. We all know that."

Duck nodded. "We do. But here's what I've been thinking. I heard they think that woman up on the mountain probably had been there a few months because of the state of the body and everything."

Paul checked the bar to make sure nobody needed a drink. "And your point is?"

"Hold on. Follow me with this. Do you remember when I was in here with Juliette a few days ago?"

"Yes."

That night she told us they all come to town the first week in May." Duck leaned back and folded his arms. "Now that would put that creepy Dieter guy in town exactly the same time that something happened to Grace, or whoever it is up on the mountain."

"So what you're telling me is that you think Dieter had something to do with the girl on the mountain and also kidnapped Rachel's sister?"

Duck's eyes narrowed. "Could be. Maybe not both, but then, who knows? We may have a serial killer on our hands. Who knows what that guy did back in Germany? All I know is, he gives me the creeps."

"Are you sure you're not dumping on this guy because you think he got you fired from your jewelry repair gig?"

"Hell no. I've been thinking about this way before that happened."

Paul smiled. "So what are you going to do about it, Sherlock?"

Duck scratched his head. "Hell if I know." He turned toward the door. "Here comes your new girlfriend. Looks like she's all excited."

Rachel burst in through the doorway and hurried over to them. "Paul, you're not going to believe this. I just came from the police station. They found where Olivia's been staying."

Duck patted the stool next to him. "Here, sit down."

"What? Is she there? Is she okay?" Paul asked.

Rachel frowned. "No. the guy that runs the place said they left Thursday night. Tommy pushed her into the car, and they took off."

"Where were they staying?" Paul asked.

"Oh, you're not going to believe it. It was the place on Turner Lane you found this morning."

Paul stepped back. "You've got to be kidding. Amazing. All because of Charlie."

Duck asked, "How did the cops find out where they were staying?"

"The deputy I talked to called Tommy's number. Tommy told him."

Duck nodded. "What happens now? What about your sister?"

Rachel sighed. "They're going to arrange for Tommy to take a lie detector test."

Paul poured a beer for Rachel. "Where did they find him?"

New York City. Right where his mother said he was."

"Do they have any idea of where your sister is?" Paul asked.

Rachel's eyes teared. "They don't know."

Paul nodded toward the door. "Look who's here."

Duck and Rachel turned. The Detective who was asking Paul questions in his apartment approached them. He motioned to Paul.

Paul stepped out from the bar.

The detective said, "I need to talk to you." He looked around. "In private."

"There's a place over here we can go to." Paul walked him back to a small office, pointed to a chair, and shut the door. "What's going on?"

"We've positively identified the body as Grace Mattson. I wanted to talk to you again to see if you've been able to think of any information that would be helpful to us."

"I knew it was Grace. I heard yesterday."

The Detective looked surprised. "Yesterday? Who told you?"

"I went over to Grace's parent's house. I wanted to talk to her mother."

Detective Neimi shifted in the chair. "Have you remembered anything you thought I should know?"

Paul shook his head. "Nothing."

Olivia leaned against the door. She had pushed, pounded, and kicked at it endless times. It wasn't going to open. She had finally got the courage to drag the bloodied mattress with Arnold's lifeless body on it to the far end of the room. Before that she had tried to knock a hole in the boards where the small sliver of light was. She had used the plastic chair to pound on the wood. Her hands were blistered and the boards weren't moving. All that work and only one small chip had broken loose.

Was this really going to be how she died? Starved to death in some tiny room where nobody would ever find her?

She was thirsty. And hungry too. She picked up the cup that was half filled with watered down Coke. Good thing she'd hoarded it. She never knew when he was going to bring something to eat or drink. How had this not spilled during their fight? Now the question was, how long could she make it last?

Was that a noise? She put her ear to the door. No, it was nothing. Just like the hundred other times she thought she'd heard something.

She glanced over at Arnold's body. That spoon had been a bad idea. At least he had been feeding her and bringing her water. Her stomach growled. But then again, he had come down to kill her. At least it would have been quick. Probably would have only taken a few minutes with that bag over her head. Not wasting away for days like what was going to happen now.

She closed her eyes. It was time for another prayer.

Chapter 22

RACHEL SAT AT the kitchen table. "After I clean up the breakfast dishes, I'm going to drive over to the place Olivia stayed and talk to the owner. You want to come with me?"

A look of disappointment crossed Paul's face. "I'm supposed to meet Charlie this morning to hear about his trip."

"Oh. Okay."

"I can tell you how to get there. Remember where the Welcome Center is for the park?"

"Yes."

"Well, Turner Lane's a mile or two before that. From what I remember, it's not much of a road and kind of hard to spot."

"Thanks. I'll keep an eye out for it."

An hour later Rachel slowed the car and made a U-turn. Paul was right. She had missed it. She turned down the narrow lane. How did they ever find this place? It was out in the middle of nowhere.

She held on tightly to the steering wheel and concentrated on the bumpy road. There was a house in the distance. She pulled up to a gravel area, parked the car, got out, and looked around. It wasn't fancy. An old two-story farmhouse. A ramshackle garage was half hidden in the woods to the left. This is where Olivia stayed? Impossible. Nobody would stay here.

She climbed the steps to the porch and stopped at the front door. There was a sign taped to the door. *Closed due to a fire. We should be reopened for business in a month or two. The management.*

That was odd. She knocked on the door and reread the sign. Rachel waited and then knocked again. After a minute or two, she peered into the window. It didn't look like there had been a fire. The place looked very tidy.

She called out, "Hello. Hello. Is anybody home?" She pounded on the door. "Hello!" Maybe someone was at the back of the house.

Rachel left the porch and circled around to the far end of the house. She walked up another set of steps and knocked on a door which looked like it opened to the kitchen. "Hello. Is anyone home? Hello." There was no response. She knocked a few more times and then retreated down the steps. She slowly walked back to the car.

The lake! How beautiful. She had been concentrating so intently on driving down the narrow road and seeing the house, she had completely missed the beautiful view of Lake Superior.

She stared out over the water. Had Olivia stood here and enjoyed the view? It had been almost two weeks now since she hadn't returned. What had Tommy done with her? She needed to talk with Deputy Kevola. When were they going to conduct that lie detector test? Tommy shouldn't be out walking the streets. He needed to be looked at more closely. He had a bad history with women, and none of Olivia's friends had a good thing to say about him. Why were they just taking his word for everything?

She turned toward the house. The roof needed repair. The whole place could use a coat of paint, and the front porch railing was missing a few spindles. Why would they stay here? None of the motels she had visited seemed to be filled up. Where was the proprietor? Where had the fire been?

She got into the car. Nothing made sense. Halfway down Turner Lane, Rachel slammed on the brakes. A deer was standing in the middle of the narrow path looking at her. It was so beautiful and graceful. Just like Olivia.

Rachel put her head down against the top of the steering wheel. Tears welled up. She pounded the dashboard. Why? Why? Why?

Paul sat with Charlie in the back booth of the Koffee Kup Kafe. He handed Charlie's phone back to him. "Great pictures. I'd like to go to California sometime. Looks like you had a good time."

"I did. Cost me a bundle, but it was worth it. It was nice seeing my sister again. But to tell you the truth, I was happy to come back home. It was a madhouse with her newborn and everything. People coming and going. Thank goodness I found that place to stay. It was nice going back to my room and having some peace and quiet."

Paul leaned forward. "Oh, I forgot to tell you. Thanks to you, we found where Rachel's sister was staying."

"What? How did I have anything to do with it?"

Paul laughed. "I was telling Rachel about you finding a place online. Rachel had checked out every motel around, and nobody had seen her sister. When I mentioned where you were staying, we looked up those internet places around here. Sure enough, that's where she had been."

"Well? Where is she?"

"They don't know. The guy that runs the place told the cops that Olivia's boyfriend forced her into the car, and they took off. But the boyfriend said they had a big fight, and he left without her."

"Somebody's lying," Charlie said. "Where were they staying?"

"Some house down on Turner Lane."

Charlie's brow furrowed. "Turner Lane? The only place down there since Turner's place burned down is the Spivey house. Nobody would stay there."

"That's where the cop told Rachel they had stayed."

Charlie shook his head. "I hope they didn't pay much."

"By the way, did you hear that they finally identified the body on the mountain?"

Charlie glanced down at the table. "Yes, I did. I didn't want to bring it up." He looked at Paul. "I didn't know Grace that well. I think I bumped into you guys a few times, but I'm sorry. I know that has to be hard for you."

Paul nodded. "I still can't believe it. I went over to her parents' house to verify that she was still in Chicago. The cops have been over at my place asking me questions about her." He paused. "Which really freaked out Rachel, but that's another story. Anyway, when I was at the house, her mother told me that it was Grace up there. They had informed her that morning."

"That has to be bad. Having your child die before you. I keep thinking of my new nephew. What would that do to my sister? Was Fred home? This has to be devastating, with his campaign and everything."

Paul hesitated. Should he tell him about the separation? "No, he wasn't there."

"I heard he built another dealership downstate."

"I heard that too."

Charlie let out a low whistle. "He must be loaded. Hell, he has to be loaded in order to run for state representative."

"You got that right."

Charlie finished his coffee. "Well, time to get over to the office. Sorry to hear about Grace. What the hell happened up there, I wonder?"

"I don't know. One of her friends told me she'd been depressed when she had to move back here. Then there's the guy she went out with after me."

"Who was that?"

"Vince Moretti. He's a hot head. I heard he hit her." Paul shrugged. "Nobody seems to know what happened to her. If you hear anything during some of your meetings, let me know."

Charlie stood up. "I will."

Paul sat alone for a few minutes thinking about what to do. He paid for the coffee's and walked out to his car. It was only eleven o'clock. He had time. Should he do it? Why not.

The large Mattson Motors dealership was on the corner of South Front Street and Capitol Drive in Marquette. Immediately Paul was approached by a smiling young man. "Hi. What can I do for you, sir? Can I put you into a brand new automobile today?"

"No, not today. I'm looking to see Mr. Mattson. Is he in?"

The young man stepped back. "Mr. Mattson? Um, I don't believe he's in today." He pointed to a highly polished counter. "Why don't you go over there? Ms. Davidson will be able to help you out."

Paul walked over to where the salesman had pointed. An attractive young woman looked up from some paperwork. "Can I help you?"

"Yes, I'd like to see Mr. Mattson for a few minutes, if possible. My name's Paul Karppenin. He knows me."

The woman pursed her lips. "I'm sorry. Mr. Mattson's up at the election headquarters right now."

"Where's that?"

"It's on West Washington and the corner of Third." She typed a few strokes on a keyboard and looked at a screen. "Do you have an appointment? I don't see anything on his calendar."

"I don't. Thank you for your time." He walked back to his car. Was this a good idea? Would he even see me? What the hell. He'd come this far.

Paul drove down Washington Street and parked in front of the building. The election headquarters was in a small storefront. Several desks and white plastic tables piled high with flyers and yard signs were visible through the front windows. Paul pulled the door open. Several heads turned in his direction.

He walked up to a man who was handing out lists of names to several young people. "Excuse me. I understand Mr. Mattson's here. My name is Paul Karppenin. I'd like a few minutes of his time, if possible."

"What's this about? He's kind of busy right now."

"I'm sure he is. Mr. Mattson knows me. I'm sure he'll say okay if you let him know I'm here."

The man sighed and set down his pile of papers. "Okay. Give me a minute." He returned shortly and said, "Okay. You can see him." He pointed. "Down the hall and to the right."

Paul walked up to the door and knocked.

"Come in."

Fred Mattson was slumped in a chair behind an old desk. He was wearing a wrinkled white shirt with the sleeves rolled up. His tie hung loose around his neck, and his hair was uncharacteristically messy. A bottle of whiskey and a small glass sat on the desk. He motioned for Paul to enter.

Paul pulled up a chair and sat down.

"If you're here to try and talk me out of putting up the car wash, you're wasting your time."

"I'm here because of Grace. I wanted to extend my condolences."

Fred poured some whiskey into the glass and drank it. "Thank you. I appreciate that. It's...a damn shame." He poured another. "You want some?"

Paul shook his head. "No, I need to be going. I just wanted to...you know, say I'm sorry for your loss."

"Thanks. It's a mess. One hell of a mess." He slid down a little in the chair, then grabbed hold of the side of the desk and steadied himself.

Paul stood up. There was no point in continuing this conversation. As he exited the election headquarters, the man who told him where the office was wouldn't make eye contact.

Duck entered Russo's Tavern and looked around. She wasn't there yet. He took a seat at the bar and asked the bartender, "Is Paul working?"

"No, he comes in at two. You're here kind of early, aren't you, Duck?"

He smiled. "Yeah. I'm supposed to meet someone. What time is it?"

The bartender turned and pointed to the clock above the bar. "Almost noon. Is it the girl who called here this morning wondering how she could contact you?"

"Yes, thanks for calling me and letting me know. Wait until you see her." Duck looked up at the clock. "Hell, it's five o'clock somewhere. Get me a Bud draft."

"Okay. One draft coming up."

"*Bonjour*, Mr. Ducky."

Duck spun around. "Juliette! I didn't see you come in."

She gave him a hug. "I'm sneaky like a cat."

Her perfume was wonderful. "I must admit, I was surprised you wanted to see me. What was so hush-hush that you couldn't tell me over the phone?"

She squinted. "Hush-hush? What is that?"

Duck thought. "Secret. It means like not telling someone."

She smiled. "Oh, there is nothing secret. I just wanted to tell you in person. Mrs. Haverhill found the missing ring. She misplaced it. She is very sorry that Dieter accused you of stealing it. She never told him to say that. She wants you to come back."

Duck drummed his fingers on the bar. "Really? She found the ring?" He took a sip of beer and thought for a moment.

Juliette took his hand. "And I want you to come back also."

"I don't think Mrs. Haverhill misplaced anything. I think that big goon, Dieter, hid the ring, accused me of stealing it, and then when I was let go, he probably slipped the ring back into the box or put it somewhere where Mrs. Haverhill would find it."

Juliette shook her head. "*Non. Non.* I don't think Dieter would do such a thing."

"Right. He couldn't stand to see us having a relationship. He's been giving me nasty looks all the time. He's a piece of work."

She squeezed his hand. "Forget about *Monsieur* Dieter. When are you coming back?"

"Well, if it wasn't for you, I'd tell them all to go to—." He paused. "How about tomorrow? Can you tell Mrs. Haverhill I'll start back tomorrow?"

Juliette leaned over and kissed him on the cheek. "*Oui.* She will be delighted."

"But if that big goon gives me any trouble, I'll—"

"He won't," she interrupted. "Do you want to have a quick bite to eat? I told Mrs. Haverhill I'd be back soon."

Duck grabbed two menus. "Sure. Let's do it."

Paul walked into the bar and spotted Duck. "A little early for drinking, isn't it, Duck?"

Duck turned. "Early for drinking? Ha. Who are you trying to kid. Where you been? You just missed her."

Paul looked around. "Missed who? Was Rachel here?"

"No, Juliette. We just had lunch. She had to race back to the mansion. I was just finishing this beer."

"Was she here to carry out a citizen's arrest?"

"Very funny. No, they want me to come back. Apparently, old Mrs. Haverhill found the missing jewelry." Duck made a fist. "I know that Dieter had something to do with this."

"Are you going back?"

"I guess so."

A man walked up to them. "Hey, Paul. What's this shit about you siccing the cops on me?"

Paul turned. "I didn't sic anybody on you, Vince. The cops showed up at my place asking questions. I would imagine they want to talk to anyone who dated Grace. Don't you ever watch TV? The boyfriends are always suspects."

"Gus said you were looking for me."

"I was."

"What's that all about?"

"I'm trying to find out what happened to Grace."

Vince took a step closer. "You think I had something to do with that?"

"I don't know what to think. I do know you pushed her around and didn't have a problem hitting her."

"Who told you that?"

Duck got up and moved to a stool a few feet away.

Paul responded, "Multiple sources. Are you telling me it's a lie?"

"I don't need to tell you anything. I didn't come over here to let you interrogate me like you're some kind of detective. I came over here to tell you to leave me out of this. What happened between Grace and me was our business."

Paul smiled. "Really? I heard that Mr. Mattson may have thought part of it was his business too."

A flush rose up on Vince's neck. "You sure hear a lot of bullshit. That man's a lunatic. He threatened me. Said he'd get a hitman to take care of me. He better watch his step. I got shit on him that he sure as hell doesn't want to get out. If he ever tries to push me around again, he'll regret it."

Duck spoke up. "I'd watch out for him, Vince. He's probably going to be our next state representative. You don't want a guy like that pissed off at you."

"Who told you that?"

Duck continued, "He's got an office set up in Houghton. A friend of mine's volunteering for him."

Vince thought for a minute. "No shit. Well, that's pretty damn interesting." He turned toward the door. "Oh, you can cross me off your list about Grace. The cops have talked to me twice, but I was in the county jail for 30 days when they think something happened to her." He smiled. "Couldn't ask for a better alibi if I tried." He pointed to Paul. "Looks like you're the only one under suspicion." He walked over to the door and stopped. "Hey, Paul. You better watch the cash register when you're buddy Duck's around. His brother told me he's quite the thief."

Duck jumped off the barstool. "Why, you little—"

Paul grabbed him and held on to him until Vince left the building.

"Man, that guy's a real ass-hole," Duck said.

Paul nodded. "He's trouble. That's for sure."

At five-thirty Rachel walked into Russo's. She sat at the bar and picked up a menu.

Paul poured drinks for a couple at the other side of the bar and then came over. "How was your day?"

"I don't know. I'm still trying to figure it out. How was yours?"

He told her about his visit with Grace's father, and then added, "Oh, and it looks like I'm now the only suspect in what ever happened to Grace."

She looked up. "Why is that?"

"Seems that bad boy Vince was in the county lockup during the time they think Grace died up on the mountain."

"You need to figure out what happened up there and do it quickly."

He nodded. "Don't I know? Anyway, did you learn anything today?"

"I finally found the place. You were right. It was hard to find. I drove right by the road the first time."

"What's it like?"

"I can tell you what it's not like. It's not like any place I'd ever think my sister would stay. It's an old, two-story farmhouse. It has a great view of Lake Superior, but it's run-down, and is out of the way. You have to drive down a narrow path through the woods for a long time just to get to it. How they ever found it is beyond me."

"What did they say about your sister? Do they remember her?"

Rachel shook her head. "No one was home. There was a sign on the front door that they were closed because of a fire."

"A fire?"

"That's what it said. I peeked in a few windows. I couldn't see any signs of a fire."

"Maybe it was upstairs."

"Could be. I sure wanted to talk to the guy who ran it. I think his name was Albert or Arnold. Something that started with an *A*."

Paul noticed her menu. "What are you having? I'm hungry too."

"I'm not sure yet, but I'm exhausted. Do you mind if I head over to your place after we eat? I need a nap."

"Be my guest."

The more Olivia tried not to think about water, the more she thought about water. How long was it going to take? Dying of thirst. Not the best way to go. When would they find her? Did Arnold's mother have any friends? Would they start to miss her after a while? Maybe come and see if she was okay. Knock on the door a few times and then leave? It could be weeks. Maybe even months. There wouldn't be much left of her by then. Would they ever be able to tell that the pile of thirsty bones had once been her?

She looked down at the broken chair leg. She didn't have the energy to pound it on the wood again. Besides, her hands hurt. She had blisters from the long hours of futile pounding. Nobody had heard. Not even the deaf neighbor who lived a mile and a half away. She lay down next to the door and drifted off to sleep.

Chapter 23

THE PHONE IN Paul's kitchen was ringing. Then his cellphone. He rolled over and looked at the time. It was six-thirty in the morning. His kitchen phone rang again. Something was up. He forced himself out of bed.

Rachel opened one eye. "What's all the racket?"

"Someone's trying to reach me. They're calling both phones." He stumbled into the kitchen and grabbed the phone.

Rachel propped herself up on one elbow and tried to listen.

"What? Vince? Where? On the mountain?"

Rachel hurried into the kitchen. One look at Paul's face told her this was serious.

Paul hung up the phone. "That was Charlie. You're not going to believe this. They found Vince up on the mountain. They think he killed himself. It was near the trailhead where they found Grace."

Rachel pulled out a chair and sat down. "So, it was Vince that killed her?"

"No, he couldn't have. He told me yesterday that he was locked up in the county jail during the time they think she died."

"Maybe he lied?"

Paul rubbed his forehead. "Why lie about that? It's easily confirmed."

"So why did he kill himself? Was he that broken up about her death?"

Paul shook his head. "I don't think he killed himself at all."

"What does that mean?"

"I'm not sure yet."

After a hurried breakfast, Paul said, "I need to talk with Grace's mother again."

Rachel glanced down at the table. "Oh. I was hoping you'd come back with me to the house on Turner Lane. I really need to talk with that Arnold guy."

"That's fine. We can do that. How about we swing by Mrs. Mattson's first. In fact, I'd like you to be there with me. I want to get your take on what she tells us. That won't take long. Then we can head over to Turner Lane."

She smiled. "Let's go."

An hour later they pulled up to the Mattson house. "Now that's a surprise," Paul said.

"What?"

"The yellow corvette. That's Grace's step-dad's car."

"What's so surprising about that?"

"Mrs. Mattson told me they were separated."

"Oh. Well, maybe under the circumstances, he's here for support."

"Maybe."

Paul walked up to the door and knocked. A corner of the living room window curtain parted, and someone peered out. The door opened. Fred Mattson stood in the doorway. "Hello, Paul. What can I do for you?"

"Can we come in? I wanted your wife to meet someone."

Fred looked behind Paul and saw Rachel. He replied, "Ah, we're in the middle—"

Mrs. Mattson stepped out from behind her husband. "It's Paul? Come in. Why are you talking outside?"

Fred stepped away, and they entered the living room.

"Please sit down," Mrs. Mattson said.

After everyone had taken their seats, Paul said, "I won't be long. I just wanted Mrs. Mattson to meet my friend Rachel. She's been in the area searching for her sister who came up here on a hiking trip and then disappeared."

Mrs. Mattson's hands flew up to her face. "She's missing? Oh. That's awful." She looked over to her husband. "Do you think it could have something to do with our Grace?"

Fred thought for a moment. "Maybe. I'm sure we'll find out soon enough what happened up on that mountain."

"Can I get you anything to drink? Coffee?" Mrs. Mattson asked.

"No thank you. We should be going. I just wanted to stop by and see you again after our long talk the other day."

Fred turned. "Long talk?"

Mrs. Mattson coughed. "Well, it wasn't that long."

Paul said, "I came by to see you both. The police were asking me all kinds of questions about Grace. I really hadn't heard much about her after she went to Chicago, so I thought I'd stop by and get caught up." He paused and glanced down at the carpet. "Um, that's when Mrs. Mattson told me about Grace. That it was her up on the mountain."

Fred stood up. "It's that Vince. He beat her up. When I found out about Grace, I called Commissioner Samperton and told him to arrest Vince."

"I thought the same thing," Paul replied. "But did you know Vince has an airtight alibi?"

Fred spun around. "Alibi? What kind of alibi?"

"He was locked up when the police think Grace died."

"Who told you that?" Fred asked.

"Vince."

"And you're going to believe him? He's a liar."

"I can't imagine why he'd lie about that. It would be easy enough to check out."

Fred paced the floor. "Grace was very despondent when she came back from Chicago. Very despondent." He stopped in front of Paul. "You broke her heart. I'll never forgive you for that."

"Fred!" Mrs. Mattson cried. "Stop it! What are you saying? Paul was wonderful to her. Grace had problems. She was drinking too much." She turned to her husband. "You know she had issues."

"This isn't the time to be discussing family matters." Fred glanced at Rachel. "In front of strangers."

"Did you know Vince was dead?" Paul asked.

Mrs. Mattson sat back. "What? He's dead? Vince?"

Paul nodded. "They found his body early this morning up near the Summit Peak Trail."

She turned and stared at her husband.

Fred snapped his fingers. "There you go. I don't care what you say about an alibi. He did it. Vince went back to the scene of the crime and killed himself. Guilt drove him to take his own life."

Paul took Rachel's hand. "We need to go."

She rose and followed him out the door.

As they approached the car, Rachel said, "That was very uncomfortable. Why did you bring me here?"

"I didn't know Fred was going to be there. I wanted to ask Mrs. Mattson something. But with her husband there, there was no way I could."

A frantic voice yelled, "Wait!"

Paul and Rachel turned toward the house.

Fred was silhouetted in the doorway as Mrs. Mattson ran after them. "Please! Don't leave. I need to tell you something."

Her husband yelled, "Patricia. Shut up. Get back here."

Mrs. Mattson joined them. As they got closer to the car, she started sobbing. "Get me out of here. I think Fred killed her."

Rachel stopped. "What?"

Paul watched as Fred disappeared into the house. "Get in the car. We need to leave now." Paul held the back door open as Mrs. Mattson climbed in.

Rachel got into the passenger seat and stared out the windshield. She pointed. "Oh my God! Watch out!"

Fred was back in the doorway. This time he was holding a gun, and it was pointed at them. He fired off a round at the car.

"Get down!" Paul yelled. A bullet smashed through the windshield and slammed into the back seat with a thud.

Rachel screamed.

Patricia sat up. "No, I'm not going to let that man kill you people or terrorize me." She threw open the door.

Paul tried to grab her. "Get down! He's going to kill you!"

She stepped outside the car. "Then let him. He's killed everything that's important to me including my daughter. I don't have anything to live for. If I'm the reason he rots the rest of his life in prison, at least my life was worth something."

She turned and walked toward him. "Go ahead, Fred. Shoot me. You abused Grace, and I pretended it didn't happen. I failed her. I don't deserve to live."

Fred took a shooter's stance with arms outstretched and both hands steadying the gun.

"Stay down," Paul whispered to Rachel. He didn't want her to see what was going to happen.

Patricia continued to walk up to her husband. When she got within five feet of him, she stopped. She crossed her arms and stared into his eyes. "Go ahead. Kill me."

Fred's arms began to shake slightly. He slowly moved the gun away from her. Then with one quick continuous motion, he swung the gun up to his head and pulled the trigger.

Four hours later, back at the apartment, Paul sat on the couch with Rachel lying next to him. He had wanted to pour himself a double shot of whiskey when they returned, but Rachel talked him out of it.

It had taken hours for them to provide statements to the police about what had happened. There was no more talk of going over to Arnold Spivey's house that afternoon. It would have to wait.

Duck stood in front of the Haverhill chateaux holding his box of tools. Juliette opened the door. "*Bounjour, Monsieur* Duck. Come in." She glanced behind and then quickly gave him a peck on the cheek.

"Where's Dieter?"

"He's outside trimming some bushes."

Duck followed Juliette to his workspace. He set his tools down. Another metal box of jewelry was waiting for him.

"I'll prepare a nice lunch for you," Juliette said.

"Can we eat together?"

She winked. "Maybe."

Duck spent the next few hours cleaning and repairing a seemingly endless supply of expensive gems.

A deep voice from behind made him jump. "Mrs. Haverhill would like to see you."

Duck turned to see Dieter looming over him. "She wants to see me? Why?"

Dieter ignored his question. "Follow me."

Duck tried to keep up as they marched through several rooms. They finally stopped at the bottom of a large staircase. Juliette was waiting on the upper landing.

Dieter motioned for Duck to go up the stairs. When he was at the top, Duck asked Juliette, "What's this all about? I hope she's not going to give me hell because she thinks I stole something."

"I do not know. She just asked me to get you." They walked down a long hallway and stopped in front of an ornate wooden door. Juliette quietly tapped twice.

A faint voice from inside said, "Come in."

As Juliette opened the door, Duck whispered, "Where does Dieter stay?"

She looked puzzled.

"Quick, where's Dieter's room?"

She pointed to where they had come from. "It's the first one on the right at the top of the stairs. Why?"

"No reason. I just wondered." He stepped into a large, dim room.

Mrs. Haverhill was sitting at a small writing desk near the far windows. She had gray hair piled on top of her head and was wearing an ornate silk bathrobe. "Sit down, Mr. Lindquist."

Duck took a seat in front of her at the desk.

"First, I want to take this opportunity to give you my sincere apology for the terrible misunderstanding that took place. I'm afraid one of my staff jumped to a very unfortunate conclusion that turned out to be devastating. Just devastating." She leaned forward. "You will accept my apology, won't you?"

Duck smiled. "Yes, certainly. Thank you for having me back."

"Wonderful. I'll find a way to make everything right. But, more importantly, I have a question for you."

Duck waited to hear what it was.

"Do you know, or are you related to, a woman named Mildred Lindquist? That was her maiden name. I don't know what her married name would be."

"Mildred? Yes, she was my grandmother."

Mrs. Haverhill smiled. "Marvelous! I'm so thrilled. Mildred and I were great friends many years ago. I knew her when we both worked in Chicago. That was back in 1957. I'm afraid we've lost touch." She hesitated. "I hate to ask you this, but is…is Mildred still alive?"

Duck glanced down at the hardwood floor. "No, she passed away almost five years ago."

A look of disappointment washed over Mrs. Haverhill. "That's too bad. She did a wonderful thing for me back then, and I was hoping I could reach out to her. When I heard you were coming here to work, I couldn't help but wonder if you were related. I knew she was from this area."

Duck smiled. "She was a beautiful lady. She appeared in many Chicago plays. She even went out to Hollywood for a few years, but that didn't work out for her."

"Who did she marry?"

"She returned to Chicago and married a man she knew there. They had a daughter and a son, my father. They've since passed. I'm the only living relative of hers now."

Mrs. Haverhill sipped from her tea cup. "I don't want to keep you from your work. It was very nice meeting you, Mr. Lindquist. Thank you for indulging an old woman and her fading memories."

Duck stood up. "It was nice meeting you too."

As he neared the door, Mrs. Haverhill called out, "Mr. Lindquist, can I trouble you with one more question?"

Duck turned. "Sure. What is it?"

"Do you know anything about this ghastly skull they found up on the mountain?"

He wondered what to say. What kind of question was that? Did she harbor thoughts about Dieter too? "From what I understand, the person they found was Grace Mattson. She was a young woman from here who had moved to Chicago and then returned. That's about all I know."

Mrs. Haverhill nodded. "I'm assuming foul play was involved?"

Duck's eyes widened. "I don't know. I heard she was depressed, but I don't think they've said anything about what actually happened to her."

Mrs. Haverhill pulled open a drawer and took something out. "Give me a minute." She turned back toward the desk and then stood up. "One of the reasons I enjoy coming back here each year is the fact that the crime rate is so low. People around here know how to treat each other."

She came over and handed him a check for five thousand dollars. "Could you please give this to the Sherriff for a reward for information concerning who may have been responsible for this?"

Duck stared at the check. "Um, yes. Sure. I'll do that."

She reached out with a wrinkled, bony hand and took his arm. "Not a word that this came from me. You understand? If he cashes this check, he must agree to my conditions. I insist that this remain anonymous."

He nodded. "Certainly. I'll tell him. Not a word. Thank you for your thoughtfulness."

"You're welcome."

Chapter 24

PAUL PICKED UP the breakfast dishes and sat down with another cup of coffee. "Did you sleep at all last night?"

Rachel rubbed her eyes. "Hardly. I kept having nightmares about Mr. Mattson. Then Olivia would come into the dream like she was his wife instead of Patricia." Rachel closed her eyes. "It was awful. I got up a few times and tried to watch TV just to get those images out of my mind." She shook her head. "You think that man killed Grace's old boyfriend, don't you."

"That's what made everything click. Vince was in the bar telling me Grace's step-dad better be careful, that he had something on him. When Vince found out he was running for office, you could see a light go on. I'm sure Vince went over and tried to blackmail Mr. Mattson. Not a good move, because Fred must have gotten the idea that Vince would be a good suspect in Grace's murder."

Rachel shuddered. "When he came outside with that gun and shot at us, I really thought that was going to be it. I can't believe Mrs. Mattson had the courage to do what she did."

"Courage? I'm not sure it was courage. I'd call it desperation and guilt, maybe."

Rachel glanced at the clock. "I'd like to get over to Spivey's place before it gets too late. We need to get there before he leaves."

Paul finished his coffee. "We can go right now. I'm just wondering if he didn't already take off somewhere a few days ago."

Rachel thought about what he had said. "I hope you're wrong. That would mean *he* did something to Olivia, not Tommy."

Her cellphone rang from the bedroom. She ran to answer it. "Hello."

"Rachel, it's Elaine."

"Oh, is everything okay?" Rachel sat down on the bed.

"Well, no. They just took your mother to the hospital. Her breathing's very labored. She's really not with it. She wasn't making any sense this morning when I stopped by to see her. The nurse and I both agreed that she needed to get to the hospital."

Rachel thought for a moment. "I'll grab my things. I'm coming home."

"Good. I think you should."

Rachel said goodbye and stuffed the phone back into her purse.

Paul stepped into the room. "That didn't sound good."

She pulled a tissue from her purse and dabbed her eyes. "It wasn't. They just took my mother to the hospital. I have to get back."

"What about the Spivey place?"

"I'd really like to talk to him, but with Mother now, I need to get back."

"Okay."

As she packed her things, Rachel tried not to completely fall apart. She was about to head home without knowing anything about what happened to Olivia. After all this time, what had she learned? Her sister had stayed in a dump in the middle of nowhere. She had either gone in the car with her nasty boyfriend, or she hadn't. If she hadn't, then where was she?

Paul carried her suitcase out to the car. He wrapped her in his arms and kissed her. "Be safe. Call me when you get home."

She blinked tears from her eyes. "I will." She got into the car and started the engine.

Paul waited for her to drive away.

The window rolled down and Rachel said, "I can't go home. I have to go back to that house. Will you come with me? It shouldn't take long. I really have to talk to that guy. Somebody's lying. Did she get in Tommy's car or not? I don't have Tommy to ask. I have to see this guy and hear what he has to tell us."

Paul bent down and kissed her. "That's what I was hoping you'd say." He walked over to the passenger side. "Let's go."

Duck drove up to the iron gate and pushed the button. Juliette's voice came through the speaker. "*Bonjour*, Duck."

The gate opened, and he drove up to the mansion. He grabbed his tools and walked to the front door. Just as he got there, the door opened and Juliette greeted him. As he stepped into the foyer, he noticed large sheets were covering most of the furniture. "What's this?"

She frowned. "We are leaving tomorrow."

His mouth dropped. "What? Leaving? Where are you going?"

"Mrs. Haverhill wants to go to her place in Rhode Island. Dieter is already on his way so he can open up the house for us."

"I just talked to Mrs. Haverhill yesterday. She never mentioned anything about leaving. What about us?"

"Her daughter is sick. She got the call last night. I will miss you. We can talk on the telephone."

"When are you coming back?"

"That is up to Mrs. Haverhill. Maybe sometime in October. She enjoys seeing the pretty colors of the leaves."

"What about all the work I still have to do?"

Juliette shrugged. "What can I say?"

As they drove down Turner Lane, Rachel pointed. "There's the place. I still can't believe this is where Olivia agreed to stay. I mean, look at this place."

Paul glanced up at the house as she pulled to a stop. "Looks like our friend Tommy was on a very limited budget." He turned to Rachel. "Okay, we have to ask this guy as many questions as we can. I want to study his reactions. But we have to be careful. Either Tommy or Arnold is a bad actor. We have a fifty-fifty chance it's this guy."

She nodded. "I know. I'm really glad you're with me."

Paul stepped out of the car. "Me too. I can't believe I let you come here the first time on your own. What was I thinking?"

Rachel followed him up the porch steps. He knocked on the door.

She pointed to the sign. "There's the note I told you about. It hasn't moved."

213

Paul knocked again, then turned to her. "When was the deputy here?"

"I don't remember if he told me what day he came out, but I think it was about a week ago."

Paul noticed the garage. "I'm going to see if there's a car parked in there."

He walked over to the run-down structure and pulled the door open. Inside was a black Chevrolet Blazer. It looked to be about six years old. He opened the driver-side door and checked inside. There was no sign of blood or anything else out of the ordinary.

He bent down and looked underneath the front seats. A box was stuffed below the passenger seat. He pulled it out and lifted up the top. What the hell did we have here? Gloves, duct tape, rope, zip ties, and a knife.

He put the top back on, slid the box back underneath the seat, and stood there for a moment. This looked bad. Who carries around shit like that? Should he mention this to Rachel? No, not yet. He needed to get back to her.

Paul exited the garage and joined her on the porch. She was peering in the window. He said, "There's a car there."

She jumped. "Shit! Don't sneak up on me like that. You about gave me a heart attack!"

"Sorry. I found a car back there. Someone may be home."

"I've been knocking on this door for a long time. The last time I was here, I went over and tried the back door."

"Let's give it a try."

Rachel led him to the back of the house. "Watch out for rotten wood on these steps." She approached the door and called out, "Hello. Is anybody home?"

Paul pounded on the door. They were greeted with silence. He said, "I don't like it. You'd think someone would be here."

"I don't know. It just seems odd. Maybe Mr. Spivey had to find a job when he shut the place down because of the fire."

"Could be, but it just seems too coincidental. Do you think when the police showed up and started asking questions, he got scared and took off?"

"I hope not. That wouldn't be good news for Olivia. Do you know the family?"

"My dad knew a Spivey that drove a truck. I don't know if it's part of this family or not."

Rachel looked through the window. "Nothing looks changed from when I was here before. That bottle of Mountain Dew was sitting in the same spot on the kitchen table. I wonder if the house is empty."

Paul surveyed the property from the back porch. "Wait a minute. Look over there in the middle of that clearing."

She turned to where he was pointing. "What? I don't see anything."

"They had a fire all right. See that burned area? That's where an old barn must have been."

"Barn!" Rachel cried out. "Was that the barn we've been looking for?"

Paul ran down the steps. "Come on. Let's go see."

As they neared the blackened area, Paul said, "This just happened recently. Look how the ashes are hardly scattered and—" He sniffed the air. "It smells like a fire." He surveyed the blackened rectangle. "This must have been quite a blaze. I wonder if the fire department came out here." He kicked a pile of burned and twisted metal. "Looks like everything inside got burned up too."

Rachel turned toward the house. "I'm going to go back there. I want to check something out."

Paul had bent down and was examining something in the dirt. "Okay."

Just before he'd pointed to the burned area in the field, Rachel noticed that the kitchen window was open about an inch.

She walked up the steps to the back porch, reached over, and pushed the window up. Carefully she climbed up onto the back porch railing and slid into the opening. The house was eerily silent. She felt the half-filled bottle of Mountain Dew. It was warm.

"Hello! Is anyone here?" She listened for an answer.

A short hallway to the right led to a closed door. Rachel tiptoed over and tried the handle. The door swung open. From the collection of perfume bottles and brushes on the dresser, it was apparent that this was an older woman's bedroom.

A folded up wheelchair leaned against the end of the bed. A closet bi-fold door was partially open. Rachel pushed on the door and stared at the crowded array of clothes.

A sudden movement, followed by a loud screech, startled her. Something crashed against her shoulder. Rachel screamed and fell to the floor. She desperately tried to free herself from a flurry of sharp needles that dug into her flesh. She pushed herself to her feet as a huge, gray cat disappeared from the bedroom. Rachel held up her hand. It was bleeding.

She returned to the kitchen, washed her wounded hand with soap, and grabbed a handful of paper towels. She sat down and tried to catch her breath. A bag of dry cat food was overturned onto the floor of an open pantry. Brown pellets littered the floor.

She went into the living room. A drawer to an antique desk was open. She pulled out a stack of folders and sorted through them. One had the name *Thomas Riggins* written in pencil on the tab. Here it was. Proof that Tommy and her sister stayed here. She read the contract. "And guest" had been added in pencil next to his name. So he had booked this by himself. Olivia must have decided to go with him after his plans had already been made.

She put down the papers and glanced up at the staircase. Why was she afraid to walk up there? If only Paul were here. Rachel took hold of the railing and slowly ascended to the second floor.

The door to the bedroom on the left was open. A small ceramic tile with the number one was glued to the door. She walked inside and looked around. The room was small, but tidy. It contained a queen-sized bed, an old dresser, a small closet, and two chairs that needed some attention. She pulled out each drawer of the dresser and looked inside. They were all empty.

She returned to the hall and entered the second bedroom. It was similar to the first, but had a beautiful view overlooking Lake Superior. She repeated her search through the dresser with the same results. Each drawer was empty.

There was a bathroom at the end of the hallway. Rachel peeked inside. Pink and blue tiles. It needed some updating. She descended the stairs and walked back through the living room to the kitchen. She went to the window and looked out. Paul was bent over poking at the ground with a long stick.

The gray cat suddenly stepped into the room. It sidled up to her and rubbed itself against her leg. She reached down and petted it. She said, "Oh, now you want to be friends? You about scared me to death. Look what you did to my hand."

She glanced over to where the cat had come from. Stairs to the basement? What was down there? No, if she had learned anything from all those horror movies she had watched as a kid with Olivia, it was that you *never* went down into the basement. Should she go back and get Paul? She petted the cat again. He'd just laugh. She'd explored all the other parts of the house. Why not the basement?

Rachel stood. "Come on, kitty. Let's get this over with."

She was surprised to see that the lights were already on when she got to the bottom of the stairs. The area was like most basements. Cluttered and damp. A small room was off to the left. Inside was a single bed and a desk. From the clothes that were scattered around, this must have been where a man had slept. Was this Arnold's room down here?

Turning back to the other side of the basement, she saw that an old oil soaked workbench was pushed up against the wall. Near the back, cardboard boxes were stacked along the far wall along with rows of old clothes on rolling racks. It smelled musty. She stopped. No this smell was different. Rachel covered her nose with her hand. It was the smell of death.

She shivered and was about to turn back when something caught her eye. A path. A narrow walkway ran between the clutter of boxes and racks of clothes. What was that? A two-by-four. Why was a two-by-four mounted on a small door?

Someone had told her that the smell of a dead person had an odor that would never be forgotten. This smell was something she had never experienced before. It was something you couldn't forget.

Rachel pressed her hand tighter against her nose and walked closer to the door. She pushed several boxes aside and

The House On Turner Lane

stared at the small door. Someone had gone to a lot of trouble to make sure this door wasn't going to open. She pushed the two-by-four up and pulled on the handle.

As the door swung open, Olivia fell backwards and landed at Rachel's feet. A rush of putrid air forced Rachel to choke back a wave of nausea. She grabbed her sister. "Olivia! Oh my God, are...are you all right?"

Olivia looked up and noticed a concerned face staring down at her. Through parched lips, she whispered, "Water. Do you have water?"

"Yes, I can get you some water." Rachel grabbed a plastic cup that was lying next to her sister.

Olivia tried to stand.

"Hold it. Stay where you are. I'll find you water someplace." She looked around. A washing machine was hooked up on the other side of the room next to a set of stationary tubs. She ran over and filled the cup.

She returned and handed it to Olivia. "Take sips. Don't drink too fast." She looked into the room and let out a scream. "What the hell is that?"

Olivia looked over to where Arnold was lying on the mattress. She didn't respond. She grabbed Rachel's hand and squeezed it tightly.

Paul stopped scraping at the dirt. He had seen enough. Those white things were bones. Human bones. Sweat broke out on his forehead. Rachel couldn't see this. He had to get her away from here and notify the authorities.

He looked back toward the house. The kitchen window was open. She was inside! If that Spivey guy was hiding in there, it wouldn't be good. He threw down the stick and sprinted toward the house.

He bolted up the porch steps and squeezed through the open window. "Rachel! Where are you?"

A faint voice responded. "Down here. I've got Olivia."

Paul spun around. Down where? He spotted the door to the basement and scrambled down the stairs. That smell. He coughed and covered his nose.

Rachel was walking toward him holding on to her sister. He ran over and supported Olivia from the other side. "How is she?"

"I'm not sure. We have to call an ambulance."

Almost half an hour later, a stream of blue Michigan State Police cars and an ambulance sped down Turner Lane. Paramedics rushed Olivia into the waiting vehicle.

Paul walked Detective Neimi over to the burned area where the bones were.

The detective kneeled. "Yep. Looks like human remains to me. More than one. No telling what the forensic unit's going to come up with here." He stood up. "I can't believe that girl's still alive. It's a miracle."

Rachel and Paul spent another hour with the police until Rachel insisted that she be allowed to head to the hospital and be with her sister.

On the drive into town, she called Elaine and told her they had found Olivia. She didn't go into any details. "I'm headed to the hospital right now."

"Hospital? Is she all right?"

"I hope so. She suffered some dehydration. We don't know how bad it is yet."

"Dehydration? Is that boyfriend there too? Did they get lost in the woods?"

"It's a long story. I'll fill you in when I get home. How's Mother?"

There was a long silence. "She's in a coma."

Chapter 25

IT WAS JUST AFTER lunch two days later when they released Olivia from the hospital. Rachel helped her into the car.

"How are you feeling?"

"Better. It's amazing what a little water can do. How's Mom?"

"I talked with Elaine this morning. She's the same."

"The police wanted me to stay longer so they could ask me more questions, but when they found out about Mom, they said I could go."

"I've got a million questions for you too," Rachel said. "But after what you went through, I'll let you tell me about it when and if you choose."

Olivia turned to the window. "He didn't rape me, if that's what you're thinking." She paused. "But, I did kill him."

"I know. Deputy Kevola told me. Let's talk about something else. You met Paul. What do you think of him?"

Olivia smiled. "He seems like a nice guy, and he's very handsome too."

Rachel turned to her. "I know. He's been so wonderful. When I came up here to see what I could find out about you, he was the only one who really listened to me and wanted to help. I don't know what I would have done without him."

Olivia teared up. "You saved my life. They told me in the hospital I only had one or two days left."

Rachel took her hand. "I almost came home that morning when I heard about Mother. Thank goodness I changed my mind."

Leslie was already sitting down when Kay entered the Koffee Kup Kafe and ran over to the table. "Can you believe it? That could have been you down in Arnold's chamber of horrors. And his poor mother. That guy was totally nuts. I knew it. I told you to watch out for Creepy Creeperton."

Leslie tried to take a sip of coffee, but her hand trembled. "It's almost impossible to believe. That poor girl. The news said they found her just in time. One or two more days and she'd have died."

"That had to be Arnold who broke into your house. He was going to kidnap you."

Leslie grabbed a napkin and wiped her eyes. "I talked with the police this morning. They showed me a stack of pictures Arnold had taken of me." She looked around. "Some of them were of us having lunch…right here!"

Kay reached out. "You're very lucky. I mean, the man was a lunatic. A complete lunatic."

Elaine jumped from her chair as Rachel and Olivia entered the hospital room. She wrapped Olivia in her arms. "Oh, it's so good to see you. We've been so worried."

Rachel walked over to the bed and took her mother's hand. "Mother, we're back. Olivia's here. She's safe. She's home now." Was that a squeeze? Had her mother just squeezed her hand?

Olivia stepped closer to the bed. "Hi, Mom. I'm home. I'm sorry I put you through all this, but I'm home now." She desperately tried not to cry.

Her mother's eyelids fluttered and then shut. She squeezed Rachel's hand again.

The nurse stepped forward. "I think this has been enough excitement for your mother for now. Let's let her rest. Why don't you come back in a few hours?"

Reluctantly, the daughters left their mother's bedside.

Charlie took a seat at the bar next to Duck. "I heard the governor pardoned you, and you went back to work over at Mrs. Haverhill's place."

"Very funny. Yeah, I went back for a total of one day. I showed up the next day, and they were shutting the place up."

"Why was that?"

"Mrs. Haverhill had to rush back out east because of her daughter or something."

Charlie motioned to Paul for a beer. "That's too bad."

Duck's face lit up. "But the day before, I got to meet Mrs. Haverhill in person."

"Really? What's she like?"

"She's very nice. It was funny. I was summoned by her like she was the queen of England. They escorted me up to her sitting room."

Charlie laughed. "What was the big occasion?"

Duck reached into his shirt pocket and pulled out an old black and white photograph. "Her." He handed it to Charlie.

"Who's that? She's beautiful."

"That's my grandmother. Mildred Lindquist. She was friends with Mrs. Haverhill in Chicago. The old lady called me up to her room to ask me about my grandmother, and to tell me Grandma had done some kind of wonderful thing for her back in the fifties."

"What had she done?" Charlie asked.

"Damned if I know. I was waiting for her to tell me, but she didn't. I wish I knew."

Charlie continued to stare at the picture.

Paul set Charlie's beer down. "What you got there?"

Charlie handed him the picture.

"Wow. Who's this? Some movie star I don't know about?"

Duck beamed. "That's my Grandma Millie. She used to act in plays in Chicago."

Paul let out a wolf whistle. "She's a beauty."

Chapter 26

ALMOST TWO WEEKS LATER, Duck walked into Russo's Tavern at eight o'clock on a Friday night. He sat down at the bar and announced in a loud voice, "For the next three hours, in celebration of the Russo building not being torn down, the drinks are on me."

Paul walked over and put his hand on Duck's forehead. "You got a fever?"

Duck pulled away. "No fever, my friend. But I did get a check for ten-thousand dollars."

Paul's eyebrows shot up. "Really? May I ask from who?"

"Mrs. Haverhill, that's who."

"Damn, Duck, you must do some magnificent work."

"If you get me a beer, I'll tell you what happened."

Paul poured him a draft. "Okay. Spill the beans."

Duck took a long drink. "It wasn't for my work. It was for two reasons. First, Mrs. Haverhill, bless her heart, felt bad that I got accused of stealing."

Paul nodded. "That was nice of her."

"And the other thing, remember when I told you that my grandma had done something nice for Mrs. Haverhill, but she didn't tell me what it was?"

"Yeah. Charlie was here when you told us that story."

"Well, yesterday I got a letter from her." Duck frowned. "Actually I got two letters, but I'll tell you about the other one later."

"And?"

"Apparently when my grandmother and Mrs. Haverhill lived in Chicago, my grandmother met Mrs. Haverhill's husband first. He fell madly in love with her, which is easy to believe from her picture. But Grandma found out that her friend liked this guy too, so she backed off.

"Turns out that the guy was loaded and provided Mrs. Haverhill with a wonderful marriage and a great life. She never forgot what Grandma did."

"What did that have to do with sending you ten-thousand bucks?"

Duck shrugged. "I don't know and I don't care."

"What about the other letter?" Paul asked.

Duck frowned. "Oh, that. I got a 'Dear Duck' letter from Juliette."

"Oh, no."

"Yeah. That damn Dieter talked her into rekindling their relationship."

"The same Dieter that you thought was a serial killer?"

Duck scowled. "Hey, I wasn't the only one who was shocked to find out Fred Mattson killed his step-daughter."

Paul raised his glass of soda. "I don't even want to think about that. Let's toast to Mrs. Mattson for canceling the car wash deal, and to you being ten thousand dollars richer."

Duck clicked his beer glass with Paul's. "I'll drink to that."

Paul leaned closer and whispered, "I've got some news too. But you've got to keep it under your hat."

"What?"

"It's about the reward Mrs. Haverhill put up."

Duck asked, "What about it?"

"The Sherriff awarded it to Rachel and me."

Duck thought for a moment. "Well, that makes sense. You two got her sister out of that hellhole."

"We're using it as a down payment to buy the bar."

Duck blurted out, "You are! That's great!"

Paul covered Duck's mouth with his hand. "Shhh. Don't say anything. We're working out all the financing details now. I don't want this to leak out until the deal's done."

Olivia and Rachel helped their mother get into bed back at the house. After enjoying the nice lunch Elaine had made for everyone, they all gathered around Joyce.

Olivia bent down and kissed her mother on the forehead. "You've certainly made a miraculous recovery, Mom. How does it feel to finally be back home?"

Joyce smiled. "I wouldn't call it a recovery, but when I found out you were back safe, I just had to try and get stronger."

Olivia turned to Rachel. "So I guess it's you I have to thank for Mom coming back home."

"That's right, and I'm never going to let you forget it."

Their mother turned to Rachel. "Are you really moving up there to be with that man?"

"That man?" Rachel repeated. "You've met Paul. You told me you liked him."

"I do, but I almost lost one daughter. I don't want to lose another one."

Rachel shook her head. "I'm looking forward to it. I'm going to be working with Paul at the same place he does. It's really not that far away. And when you say you're losing a daughter, I think the circumstances are a little different. Once Olivia gets to know Paul a little better, I'm hoping she figures out what makes a great boyfriend. Not that—"

"Okay, girls," Elaine interrupted. "I don't think we have to rehash that conversation again."

"Thank you!" Olivia replied. "I think I've learned a long, hard lesson. It's going to be quite some time before I run off to the wilderness with someone I hardly know."

James R. Nelson

ACKNOWLEDGEMENTS

To Julie Beam, Duncan Hebbard, Gordon Anderson, and Dave Hohenstern for their continued support, beta reads, editing prowess, and dedication. Your efforts are very much appreciated.

And to the best critique group there is – Gene Vlahovic, Chris Jensen, Kathryn Flanagan, Peggy Insula, and Cindy Foley. Your wit and brilliant input make this solitary endeavor so much fun.

OTHER BOOKS BY JAMES R. NELSON

The Stephen Moorehouse Mystery Series
The Butterfly Conspiracy
The Peacock Prophecy
Menagerie of Broken Dreams

The Archie Archibald Detective Series
A Crimson Sky for Dying
The Black Orchid Mystery
Unsafe Harbor

Stand Alone Titles
The Maze at Four Chimneys
The Pilot
Peacock Redux and Other Stories

James R. Nelson
Email - jrnfl@hotmail.com
Website - jamesrnelson.com